Sarah Kades
Claiming Love

CLAIMING LOVE
BY SARAH KADES

This is a work of fiction. The characters, incidents, places and dialogue are created solely from the author's imagination or used fictitiously. Any resemblance to actual persons, living or dead, events, or locales is entirely coincidental.

www.sarahkades.com

Second Edition

ISBN: 978-0-9916981-2-7

Dear Reader,

I am happy to release the second edition of my first novella, *Claiming Love*. It was a delight to write and it changed my life in truly beautiful ways. I hope you enjoy reading it as much as I enjoyed writing it.
Happy Reading,
Sarah Kades

Acknowledgements

Shelley, you opened up the world of writing to me. Alberta Romance Writers' Association, you are a wonderful writing community with depth, knowledge and dedication. Lorraine Paton, Deb Smith and June Baxter, critique partners extraordinaire, you teach me how to up my writing game every single time and what I have learned from you all contributed to this second edition. Tania Therien, your knowledge, support and complimentary approach to all things writing is an incredible amplifier. To my new friends at the Calgary Association of Romance Writers of America, thank you for the immediate welcome, sharing knowledge, and a love of making dreams come true. My family and friends, your love and support is pure energy.
Thank you.

Dedication

To James, I love every adventure with you.

Claiming Love

Prologue

Michael quickly rapped his knuckles on the oak door and entered the lush suite. Gaia was seated crossed legged on the plush green couch hunched over an ethereal laptop, frowning. She glanced up when he entered and shot him a quick smile, casting the already bright room into a radiating glow.

"Tell me good news," she said in greeting.

"The sun came up this morning."

"I know that." Gaia rolled her eyes good-natured.

Michael shrugged. "Not a lot of good news out there."

"I know that too," the Goddess answered glumly.

He tried again. "Bodin's finally coming along, that's something."

Gaia perked up at the archangel's words. She moved the laptop aside and directed her full attention to the Archangel.

"He didn't scare anyone, try to maim anyone or resort to any physical destruction on his last assignment." Michael continued, "He did swear, threaten, and was his usual pain-in-the-ass self, though."

She frowned again. "For the most part, the Changeling Program has been a success. Bodin's an outlier, that's for sure. I doubt he'll ever claim his wings."

"Outlier, that's a nice way to put it. Yeah, angels don't tend to try and browbeat people, bad for the whole free will thing." Michael saw Gaia smile at his uncharacteristic description. He was rarely sarcastic, but Bodin had a way of bringing it out.

"I'm glad he's starting to come around though, well, if you can call it coming around. Something special is about to come up," Gaia said, her voice ringing with anticipation and delight.

Michael raised his eyebrow in question. Gaia just smiled, while she started putting possibilities and doorways in place, her divine face intent and concentrating. He recognized the look but asked anyway. "A hint?"

She shook her head and gave a small smile, but said nothing as she maintained her concentration and continued her divine aligning. Michael shrugged, unsurprised. Gaia was not in the habit of talking about that aspect of her work. Still, he wondered. As head of the Angel Realm, he was responsible for, and cared about, all the categories of angels. That included the gruff, reluctant Changeling. Although a pain in the butt, Bodin had really grown on him. He was curious what Gaia had in mind and wondered if Bodin would take the latest opportunity that was presented.

Chapter One

Elle wasn't usually patient, but she could wait in the Calgary International Airport all day. Even listening to the nearby kid throwing a tantrum was better than the alternative, with how she was feeling, it felt like the kid was foreshadowing. Maybe the he knew something no one else did. If Elle was listening to a screaming kid in an airport it meant she wasn't airborne in a plane. It was ridiculous, but flying scared her.

She fiddled with the cinch cord on the bottom edge of her fleece jacket and silently chastised herself. Get a grip, everything is fine. Focus already, you're technically at work. Being scared of flying had that effect on her, it tied her up in knots. A waft of premium fresh-brewed coffee teased her nose, the smell distracting her for a moment. She loved coffee. Her thermos was as beat-up as her backpack and just as loved. She loved landscapes, too. They called to her in a way that people did not. She liked people, of course, and considered herself very lucky to have the close friends she did. But being outside in the natural world soothed her soul in a way that no other relationship ever had. She felt connected with the land in a way she could not connect with most people. Outside she felt whole, more herself.

The final boarding call for Fort McMurray, Alberta sounded. Elle took a deep, steadying breath and stood up. It was go time. At least the kid had stopped crying and was now bouncing up and down, ready to go. Maybe that was a good sign. She slowly made her way to the diminishing line. She nervously toed her well-worn work boot against the durable airport carpet and tucked a wayward blond curl behind her ear. Despite her anxiety, she smiled to herself at her footwear, taking in every scuff and snag. She had logged a lot of miles in these boots. They had taken her through some of the most beautiful parts of the country. It was a definite job perk to see all those incredible places. Sure, she had to do her job, but as an archaeologist, Elle got to survey extraordinary places. And she had to take planes for a lot of the jobs . . . Oh crap. Here came the nerves. *Deep breaths. It's an hour flight only, you can do this, Elle firmly told herself. You can do this.*

Some of her friends had been only half-teasing when they told her she should take sedatives before she flew. She knew they meant well, but she wanted to work through her fear, not medicate it. She'd arm wrestle herself into a Zen-like state, yet. She almost laughed out loud at the contradiction. At least, scared shitless, she still had her sense of humor. Besides, millions of people flew every day, zipping off to cool places all over the world, and they were just fine. She would not be stuck in fear. She would not!

If she were honest with herself, she would love to be a bush pilot. One could see so many cooler, out-of-the-way places. She just had to get a grip on her fear. And completely change her personality to quit her job and take the chance. A wistful sigh escaped her. Sometimes, she wished she were stronger, more daring. There were so many wonderful chances and opportunities a person got in life. She didn't want to be haunted by not doing something. For the most part, the only regrets in her life were the things she didn't do. Well, with the painful exception of Jay. What a stupid, stupid mistake that had been. How could she ever have been attracted to such a lame loser?

For the hundredth time since Jay, she assured herself she would wait for Matthew McConaughey's cosmic twin. She didn't know if there was such a thing as a cosmic twin, but it sounded like a good idea. Elle wondered idly if world peace could ever be achieved through beauty. If so, Matthew had a civic duty to the world to never put a shirt on again. She knew she was just being silly, but she could work with that. Just plain silly beat scared silly.

Elle walked down the moveable hallway to board the plane and tried to distract herself with daydreaming about her favorite film star. When she approached the plane, though, the knots in her stomach tightened considerably. Even Matthew couldn't block out the fact she was a few steps away from boarding a giant hunk of metal that was launched into the air, on purpose. Her rational mind understood how planes flew, but it was the rest of her that thought it was a miracle every time. Elle's spiritual preferences ran more along the forest line than cathedrals, but she did believe there was something divine and godlike out there. So, she had no problem saying a quick petition or prayer to the divine, or angels, or whoever in the universe was in charge of seeing travelers and airplanes safe and sound.

Elle silently asked, "Hey, it's me, Elle. Divine, or God, or Angels, or whichever benign, happy Being listens to 'fraidy cat travelers, please guide this plane safely to our destination." As she stepped onto the plane she continued, "Please, help me not be so scared. I really gotta work on that." As an afterthought, she added, "If it's in the cards, could I please meet a non-loser, preferably intelligent, funny, hot man, who is head-over-heels in love with me, and who I am completely smitten with, too, and in awe at the absolute raw chemistry between us?" It didn't hurt to ask.

Smiling at the flight attendant, she showed him her boarding pass before she continued the slow shuffle to her seat in the very last row of the plane. The smile was real, fear was no excuse to be grouchy. She wished she would have grabbed a cup of coffee, and maybe a side of balls, too. She snickered to herself. She did have balls. A nice pair of ovaries, tucked safely inside, right there next to her uterus. So they didn't clang when she walked, but that was okay. Good grief, her mom would freak if she knew what Elle was thinking. Not very ladylike at all. Then she'd pester about when she was going to get grandkids as long as they were talking about Elle's ovaries and uterus. *Not yet, Mom, not yet.* Elle had her hands full figuring out how to not date assholes or pass out in fear on airplanes.

****

Bodin rubbed his hands over his face and drew a deep breath. "What's my next assignment?"

He waited wearily for Michael to answer. He hated this game. Finally the archangel asked, "Why are you still here?"

Bodin looked up annoyed. "What's my next assignment?" he asked again, this time with an edge to his voice.

Michael's gaze was patient. Bodin knew the archangel was waiting for a more appropriate reply. Bodin scowled again. He stood up abruptly and started pacing. If he thought pouting would help, he might stoop to it. He'd been in this predicament for nearly a thousand years. When his best friend, only friend if he was going to be honest, had died as a Changeling, Bodin had taken his place in his grief and guilt. He still felt responsible for Eric's death, and he doubted another thousand years would make the pain or guilt go away. No one had understood why the two had been friends, let alone best friends. Eric had been light to Bodin's dark. Eric had smiled and laughed, and Bodin, even then, just scowled.

"You know why I'm still here," he ground out, glaring at the head of the Angel Realm.

"Honor to a friend. Noble, indeed, but how long are you going to go through the motions? Changelings have responsibilities, and upward mobility is one of them. You've never claimed your wings, and your heart is not in it. You barely tolerate the idea of love, and that's what we work with and from."

Bodin ignored the comment on his lack of wings, instead answered, "Love? That's bullshit. Love is what got Eric killed."

"I thought you blamed yourself for Eric's death." Michael's rational question irritated Bodin.

"Shut up."

Michael answered with a raised black eyebrow, his eyes declaring Bodin an insolent arse.

"I suck at this angel crap," he bellowed, but ducked his head at the shameful behavior.

"Yes, you do. Again, why are you still here? I know you loved Eric like a brother, but—"

"I have loved no one," he interrupted on a roar.

Michael rolled his eyes in impatience. "Seriously, you'd try the patience of the Goddess herself."

Just then, the energy shifted and Gaia appeared.

"Yes, he does. But, Michael, you don't have to point it out."

"Sorry, Mum." Michael's face was radiant in the presence of the divine. Bodin couldn't blame him.

He stared, dumbfounded, as usual, at the Goddess. Looking at her, he could almost believe love existed. She just felt good to be around. He vaguely wondered if any woman on Earth could make him believe in love. *Where did that thought come from?* He frowned and instead turned toward Gaia. Her smile was gentle, and it made him feel exposed, vulnerable. Over the years, he could always lie to himself, but he couldn't pull one over her.

"You were inquiring," Gaia said, still grilling him with her gentle, powerful smile, "as to your next assignment. Her name is Isobelle Cody, or Elle, as her friends call her. She's afraid of flying, and you're going to help her."

Bodin swiftly turned toward Michael, and then back to the Goddess, saying nothing.

Gaia raised her eyebrows, but kept talking, "As usual, you can utilize her main guardian angel, if you want or need to. Her name is Molly."

Bodin snorted. He worked alone.

Gaia continued to brief him and finished with, "And be nice."

"I'm always nice." He prepared for the zap on his tongue at the lie and wasn't able to suppress a grin. Gaia made him smile. It had taken a few hundred years, more from his stubbornness than anything else. But he didn't like showing it. He even liked Michael. He just didn't like admitting that, either. It might ruin their gruff exchanges. Being around pure love all the time had a way of wiggling into one's defenses.

Bodin was sure he was the only Changeling in history to require a thousand years and counting. Michael was right. His heart was not in it. He was quite certain he didn't have any heart left, so Michael's observation was no big surprise. It was guilt and honor that made him make that life-changing decision all those years ago. He really had no desire to be an angel or even to help his fellow man. People were largely assholes. Himself included. Eric was the only person he had ever met as a human that wasn't. Sure, the last several centuries had given him opportunity to see a different side of humanity, a better side, but he was too stubborn to admit it. Bodin was likely the loneliest angel in training out there, and the grumpiest. Gaia wanted him to be nice, ha! He had no idea how to be nice. *All right, time to get this thing done.*

****

Gaia and Michael watched Bodin leave. Concerned, Michael turned toward the Goddess. He knew the internal demons Bodin faced. Being an archangel gave quite a bit of insight. He just wondered how long the Changeling was going to live in his self-imposed purgatory. His mouth twitched into a half smile. Changelings were human angels-in-training, and few would consider the high honor purgatory.

"What aren't you telling me?" Michael asked mildly, trusting Gaia's decision. "I usually cover fear issues, or have input in them."

"I know." Gaia paused. "And I appreciate your trust."

"You are the Goddess."

"Yes, but love doesn't take anything for granted. Know I appreciate you. Elle is a doorway for Bodin, as he is one for her. Now, we just have to see if they walk through. Besides, as gruff as he is, Bodin will come to you if he needs help. He doesn't jeopardize people for ego."

Gaia looked lost in thought a moment before she smiled again, her eyes positively twinkling.

Michael was amused and curious at the extra radiance. "What?"

"Elle had another request." The goddess twirled in a circle. "I'll let Bodin figure that one out on his own, though."

Chapter Two

Elle sat with her seat belt fastened, hands folded in her lap, and her eyes closed. To anyone who chanced to glance back at her in the last row, she was sure she appeared in a peaceful catnap. Inside, she was anything but serene. In the past, she had tried keeping herself busy on planes by reading or working on a crossword, but now they just made her jitters worse.

She tried to let her mind wander. Images of hurtling through the air in a series of gigantic chunks of metal screwed together with . . . with . . . mere screws came to mind. Elle tried to control her imagination, as the thought that screws were the same things that hold together insignificant things like curtain rods or mall signs shot through her head, invading the fragile peace she was working so hard to establish. *Oh crap,* she thought, her breath coming in rapidly again. Forcing herself to take deep breathes, Jay crept into her thoughts. Great. Today, she seemed capable of two gears only, her fear of flying and Jay. She wanted to give neither any mental air time. *How in the hell am I going to get to my happy place for this flight?*

Elle suddenly opened her eyes in instinctive awareness. Blinking, she focused on the tall man standing in the aisle. He was frowning at the empty window seat, then at her.

"Pardon me," the tall, attractive stranger growled.

She wished he hadn't opened his mouth. He'd looked way better before he barked. Who yelled at complete strangers? For no reason at that? Didn't he know she was trying to stay in her *happy place?* She tried to glare at the man, but a half smile appeared for a heartbeat. Who was she kidding? Even barking, he looked pretty damn good. His black hair was long enough to be tousled, and his eyes were a sharp green. Those green eyes were currently scrutinizing her, pinning her with their intensity. He was about six-two and built like a Beamer M3, lots of power and muscle in a sleek package. She doubted he was sculpted in a gym, though. He was too real.

****

Bodin plopped down in his seat in frustration. Of course, this was his assignment. Gaia was playing hardball. Ms. Isobelle Cody was a knock out. Freakin' deities and their meddling. He knew the Goddess was concerned about him, but sending him to aid this, this siren, wasn't going to help. Gaia wanted him to learn to love, Bodin didn't believe in it. End of story.

Now lust, that was another matter altogether. He was still enough human to know exactly what lust was all about. And speaking of lust, his dick was hard. Great, he thought, full of sarcasm. That should help with the assignment, no problem. He couldn't remember the last time he was hard. What was Gaia setting him up for that he got hard just brushing past Ms. Cody? He was supposed to be a goddamn angel-in-training. The Goddess sure had a sense of humor or a really unexpected mean streak. He wondered what Isobelle's deal was. Gaia would not play with a person's affections or intentions to appease her ends. He'd just have to find out the alluring Ms. Cody's story.

Distantly, he heard the flight attendants finish their

safety demonstration. He inhaled deeply and tried to forget that the woman beside him was gorgeous and made him feel very alive and very male. Instead, his finely tuned sense of smell picked up the light scent of her soap, and the underlying mix of hormones and pheromones. Fear was in there, but Bodin was more interested in the rest. She smelled great—primal, powerful, alive, heavenly, real. So much for composure.

"You don't wear deodorant." Bodin was disgusted with himself for noticing her enticing, organic scent.

She snapped her head up to sizzle a glare at him. He watched in fascination while a myriad of emotions whizzed across the lovely woman's face. Shock, anger, regret, and confusion were there. As the plane accelerated for flight, fear appeared again. She was a fantastic creature. So honest and fresh. Bodin was human enough to be pleased when he saw the regret and confusion. She liked him, or more appropriately, could like him.

The plane lifted into the air, and he watched her take deep, focused breaths. She sat rigid, holding her athletic body in extreme attention. He felt for her suffering. *Wait a minute,* he thought. *That can't be right.* He didn't feel things for people. He just accomplished assignments. *Crap. Gaia, what did you get me into now? Feeling things, hah! Focus on the assignment,* he ordered himself. Watching the woman again, he felt his resolve start to slip. He actually wanted to be charming and soothing, not browbeat her, which was his usual way of assignment completion. And where the hell had his hard-on gone, too? Sixty seconds ago, he'd wanted to fuck her, and now he wanted to comfort and hold her. What the hell was happening to him?

"I meant that as a compliment, about the deodorant," Bodin said with sincerity, trying not to think about why he wanted her to like him and not think he was a jerk.

She looked up, disbelief clear on her face. "I know what I smell like. And I know it isn't pretty," she said through gritted teeth before focusing straight ahead again, her chest rising and falling heavily.

She stole a quick glance his way. Then a second. *She's distracted, but definitely interested.* Bodin relaxed a little and didn't even care.

"You smell earthy, real," he murmured, entranced by her neck, and wanting suddenly to nuzzle it. "Your scent reminds me of a forest in northwestern Ontario that is still quite wild, almost untouched. When it is wet, the rain makes the trees heady. The scent of the mosses and soils and barks are earthy and real. It is a place where you can get lost in your own soul." He searched her clear blue eyes. "If you let yourself."

Bodin wished he hadn't given up on his soul years ago. He wanted very much to believe he had one, and had a chance to connect to this woman's. But this was her story, for her wishes, not his. He continued to gaze into her stunning blue eyes. Willing himself to look away but failing. He wanted her, wanted everything with her. He felt himself slipping down the scree slope of infatuation. Yes, that must be what it was. Infatuation. He felt lightheaded and wonderful for the first time, well, ever. What the hell?

He couldn't stop staring. He had started this little conversation to get her mind off being scared and if he could enjoy some sensual banter with the woman, all the better to pass the time during the assignment. It had been a while, like centuries. He had not expected to get caught up in the moment, in her. She was exquisite to him. Even scared and cranky, her energy was incredible. She radiated a warm and happy energy that was open and honest. Few people did, Bodin knew. Reading energy was one of the tools Changelings were quite adept at. He felt her pull heavier than gravity.

All of a sudden, he was no longer aware of their surroundings. Bodin felt like a moon or more appropriately a hapless piece of space debris pulled into the orbit of a bright star, much bigger, stronger, and way more exciting than he was. For the first time in his life, he was floating in a moment, completely surrendered to the experience. A small corner of his mind registered that he liked it, at least this particular moment. When he saw a small smile spread across her beautiful lips, he thought he was going to explode.

"Sounds nice," she finally answered, her voice dreamy.

Bodin forgot what they were talking about.

Hitting a patch of turbulence, the plane jolted violently. Bodin immediately snapped out of his uncharacteristic revelry. Crap. In Gaia's briefing, he knew Air was active today, knew there would be turbulence, but the timing could have been a lot better. Bodin knew they were fine, the flight was fine, the pilots and equipment capable and fine. But the woman sitting in terror next to him didn't know that. She was gripping the seat's armrests so hard that her forearms and fingers were as tight as guitar strings.

Bodin thought quickly, assessing if knowledge or cooing would calm her. He chose knowledge and hoped he wouldn't get his tongue zapped in warning for talking out of school. "Scheduled turbulence of a sort." He placed his warm hand over her clenched one.

He saw her risk a quick glance in his direction. She winced when the plane hit another big bump. Crap, knowledge wasn't going to be fast enough. He tried another angle. "Ever get restless?"

This time she looked at him as if he were nuts.

"You know, restless. Jumpy. Caged." Bodin read the direction her mind went, jumpy as in plane and caged as in stuck in a plane while it tossed around on the air. Her eyes were the size of saucers of full of panic. He continued in a rush, "Not like that. I mean like you need to go do something active."

Bodin thought of sex. Lots and lots of hot, sweaty sex, a million different ways between the two of them, and hoped she picked up on the powerful vibe to trip up her brain from the scared panic loop it was running on.

It worked. He could tell the instant the scenes started flashing through her mind. Her eyes were still saucers, but now of curiosity, passion, and heat. The bumps of the plane would snap her mind back to fear, but he kept up the mental movie of hot kisses in the rain; of bodies straining against each other under the magic of moonlight; of rolling on beds of soft mosses as his face pressed into her lush breasts; of warm, sun-kissed water swirling around lip-kissed hips as he bucked into her. On and on the scenes went, each one steamier and needier than the last.

Bodin felt the energy radiating from her athletic body. She had been rigid in fear when the turbulence started, but as the scenes heated up, she was squirming in her seat. He felt the lightning energy of her release and wanted to wrap his arms around her and crush her to him.

Abruptly, he tried to reign in the impulse. He was an angel-in-training for god's sake, on assignment, no less. But, what in the hell had just happened? He gazed down at his assignment's satisfied, lovely face, her eyes closed in contentment.

Bodin knew he was in trouble, then. He wanted more.

Chapter Three

The plane was calm again, riding on smooth air. Elle floated back into her body. She stretched in pleasure. *Hmm.* She didn't want to open her eyes. She felt wonderful, so good right now, right here. *Hmm,* she stretched again. It had been awhile for her, too long, she thought. A satisfied sign escaped her. Bodies were made for that.

She hoped he'd had as good a time as she did. Embarrassed, she realized she had been so wrapped up in her own pleasure, she didn't know if he had a good time or not. Wait a minute. *He who?* Elle's eyes snapped open, and she saw the seat in front of her. She was still on the plane. Still in the air. She looked down. She was still clothed. She turned her head and saw the confused, awkwardly smiling man next to her.

"What just happened?" She whispered and darted her eyes to one side, then the other, and hoped only the man responsible knew of her satiated state.

"I'm not entirely sure." He rubbed his hand over his face, like he was embarrassed. "You were so scared during the turbulence, I tried talking to you to get your mind off it, but it wasn't working so I thought maybe you'd pick up on a steamy vibe enough to calm down and ride out the turbulence. I didn't think I misjudged your, er, appreciative glances earlier." He closed his eyes a heartbeat. "I didn't expect . . . I didn't know . . . Crap, you just clicked into me so completely. Sorry. Just sorry."

Elle was charmed. She was still feeling the warm

glow of her climax and was more than a little turned on by his sweet, pensive apology. "I still don't quite understand what just happened, but it's kinda hard to be mad at you when you just gave me more pleasure with your mind than I ever had physically. Oh my god, did I just say that out loud?" She felt herself turn eight shades of red and grimaced in embarrassment. "Besides, you did help me get through that turbulence," she added, wanting to disappear. *By creating a whole other kind of turbulence.* She was getting hot again just thinking about it.

Elle wondered if those mosses he had talked about would make a good bed while the two of them explored each other completely, physically, not just mentally. Each new bared piece of skin an adventure, a conquest, and a surrender, all at the same time. She looked at the extraordinary man who had spoken calmly and seductively about forests and with a heat in his eyes that revealed he was comparing her to those luscious wild places.

She felt like a forest nymph, beautiful and erotic. No one had ever made her feel like that.

His face went from gruff to relieved. Elle studied it now. His mouth and lips were full. The color a soft red that men never notice and women spent good money trying to replicate. His cheekbones were full and high. His chin and jaw, square. He had a wide forehead with black hair spilling across it. A small smile spread across her lips when she thought of the length of his hair. *You could run your fingers through and get a good fistful, like say in the throes of passion.* His eyes were a brilliant cut of green, hard and glittering and, at the moment, filled with wonderful promises.

He had rocked her completely, and she wanted him again. Physically. She wanted to please him, to make him writhe in powerful ecstasy. She noticed where his jacket was open. The expanse of T-shirt clad chest looked hard and powerful, and way too appealing. Her fingers itched to touch him there, everywhere. *Get a grip.* On a sigh she attempted to pull herself together. She didn't have sex with strangers. Well, never before today, and that was mental sex, so she wasn't sure if it counted. No one had ever made her curious or interested enough to share something so intimate, so quickly. This strange and wonderful man did. He still was.

"I'm Bodin."

Elle focused on the confident, friendly tone and shook his strong hand. She was relieved at the interruption. "I'm Elle. Isobelle really, but everyone calls me Elle." Unsure what to say, she went for polite query. "Are you here for work?"

"You could say that." He glanced out the plane window.

"I suppose everyone's here for work. The Oil Sands aren't exactly a vacation destination." Still embarrassed, she fidgeted in her seat, not knowing how to act after such an intimate experience with a complete stranger. "I haven't always been scared of flying. Just the last few years." She tried again for normal, but her mind kept replaying the vivid, exciting images of her and Bodin. She liked his name, liked him, liked his imagination. *Focus!* She scolded herself. "What do you do?"

"I'm a pilot."

Elle turned red again. "Wow, of course you are." Hiding her face in her hands, she mumbled, "This is so embarrassing."

He eased her hands away from her face. He hesitated a moment, before he brought them to his lips and kissed each one. "Why are you embarrassed with my job?"

"Because I'm scared of something you do every day. You're clearly safe and fine, and—ooh, keep doing that." Elle nearly purred when he continued to kiss her hands with great care.

"What were you saying?" He asked between kisses.

"Hmm? Oh, I don't know." She sank into the kisses and loved the feel, but wished he would explore other areas of her body, too. "What were we talking about?"

"Does it matter?" Bodin asked, still kissing her but letting his lips roam up her arms.

"No." Without thinking, Elle reached for his chin and directed him to her lips. The kiss started slow, both exploring the other, but swiftly turned hot and consuming. She wanted more. The thought shocked her and snapped her out of the kiss. She had just grabbed the guy and kissed him, and she was nearly crawling all over him. What was with her? Her libido was in overdrive. Mental sex was one thing, but pawing a complete stranger on a commercial jet was another. She didn't do stuff like this! What the hell happened to her inhibitions?

"Sorry. I can't believe I just grabbed you. Sorry!" She stammered, ashamed of her behavior but wanting to kiss him again. And again, and again. Good grief, good thing they were landing soon, or he was in serious danger of her pulling his zipper down, straddling his lean hips, and finding out what all the Mile High fuss was about.

Stop it! she screamed at herself. Good grief, she seriously had to buy a vibrator. With a mind of their own, her eyes roamed down his flat, T-shirt-clad torso and settled on his crotch. The telltale bulge in his jeans made her wet on the spot.

"You can grab me anytime you want." The heat in

Bodin's eyes promised everything. "You set me on fire and then keep adding flames."

Elle forgot to breath. She stared at him, mesmerized. Abruptly, the captain's voice came over the speakers and informed them that they were starting their final descent. She was grateful for the distraction. He took her hand then, in a simple caress, while the plane landed.

She didn't want him to let go.

Chapter Four

"Well, thanks again." Elle hefted her giant duffle bag over her shoulder. "You're fun to travel with. Embarrassing, but fun."

Bodin smiled, then immediately frowned. Elle's eyes twinkled, and she reached across and rubbed the frown lines on his forehead. "I'm the scaredy-cat—what are you frowning for?" Realizing her boldness, she snatched her hand away. What was it about this guy that dropped her inhibitions?

He reached for her dropped hand and squeezed it. Elle stared down where their hands touched and wished she were a different woman, more daring, less caring of what other people thought, and more willing to accept her true identity. A part of her wanted to parachute out of planes and cliff dive and to make crazy wild monkey love to one incredible stranger who gave her a glimpse of her real self with one smoldering glance. She struggled with herself and with what she had already done with Bodin. The person she put forth to the world was a tempered, tame version of the hellcat she knew was inside. She didn't want to be ruled by guilt or shame, but it was there all the same. What was happening to her?

"Elle, over here!"

She turned to see Aaron waving at her across the crowded baggage carousel area. She raised her other hand in acknowledgement, then slipped it into her pocket. It was safer there. She felt the smooth texture of her business card.

"That's my ride." She didn't want the conversation to end and toyed with Bodin's fingers with the one hand she allowed the luxury.

As if reading her mind, Bodin said, "I'll see you again."

"Hope so." Elle still hesitated.

"You don't want to kiss me with your friend watching, do you?" He asked, sounding amused, but gentle.

She wasn't surprised at his insight. "No. No, I don't. Too many questions I don't have the answers for."

She hoped Aaron couldn't see their hands. Elle looked down one more time at their entwined fingers before lifting her eyes to meet Bodin's incredible green ones. "Thank you," she said sincerely.

She held onto him with one hand and felt the temptation of her business card with her other. *Nothing ventured, nothing gained.* With a deep breath of courage, she slipped it out of her pocket, tucked it into his front jeans pocket, and dashed off. She was afraid she would do something really embarrassing like wrap her arms around that sexy neck of his and smack her very hungry lips to his very sculpted ones. The earlier taste of him had simply whetted her appetite.

Making her way through the throng of people in the crowded airport, she envisioned throwing down her bags and jumping into his arms, wrapping her legs around his hips and everything. Kissing the breath out of him and then kissing it back in. Taking her tongue and tracing his neck up to his ear, playing peek-a-boo in his ear and loving the taste of him.

"Hi, Elle. How was your flight?"

She snapped back to reality and turned toward Aaron. His broad shoulders, wavy, blond hair, and warm, brown eyes always drew appreciative stares. No doubt he was classically handsome and an absolute puppy dog. His friendly eyes and smile made people forget just how big his biceps were. He was also her best friend and co-worker.

Feeling guilty, she plastered on what she hoped was an innocent smile. "Fine. It was fine."

"I heard people talking about the turbulence and hoped you were okay." Aaron took the large duffle bag from her.

Elle and Aaron had gone to graduate school together and had worked together in the field for years, both academically and as consultants. He knew she wasn't a fan of flying.

"Oh the turbulence. Yeah, we got bounced around quite a bit."

"Well, you look pretty good for a crappy flight. Want to grab supper in town or at camp?"

"Camp, if that's all right. I've got loads to do tonight to be ready for tomorrow morning." Elle secretly smiled to herself. If Aaron only knew how fabulous that flight had been and that part of her agenda tonight consisted of fantasizing about all those images of her and Bodin.

"No problem. I got your e-mail and picked up the extra supplies already."

Aaron continued to fill her in on the project status. She tried to listen, but her mind kept wandering. She looked back to catch one more glimpse of Bodin before they walked out of the airport. She saw him, and their eyes locked. She sucked in a breath, unnerved and hot all at the same time.

"You okay?" Aaron deftly dodged a reuniting couple.

"What? Oh, yeah, I'm fine, just tired," she lied. Elle knew Aaron didn't believe her for a second.

****

Bodin watched Elle's departing back and reached for his pocket. He pulled out the slightly bent business card with the reverence of holding new life. It felt like his new life, if he was mindful, careful, and figured out how in the hell to not screw it up.

He couldn't remember ever feeling this light before. It was an intoxicating experience, and he wanted to explore it more. He wanted to explore her more, every fascinating inch of her. Bodin was grateful the plane had landed when it did. He wasn't sure how long he would have been able to last sitting next to Elle and not in her. His fabled self-control had deserted him. He would care later.

Right now, he needed to talk to Gaia and Michael. With a blink of his eyes, he disappeared.

****

Aaron turned back in the direction Elle had come from. He saw the tall man she had been standing very close to, holding something small in his hand before he just disappeared. Aaron scanned the area quickly. The tall man was nowhere to be seen. *What the ...?* Aaron looked around the small airport almost frantically. The guy was gone. Shaking his head, he hiked Elle's large duffle bag higher onto his shoulder and stepped into the brisk air, hoping his eyes were playing tricks on him. He needed a coffee.

"Who was that guy you were talking to?" He asked while they crossed the Fort McMurray Airport parking lot. He was curious what she would divulge.

"Oh, just the guy I sat next to on the plane." Elle

blushed and sounded sheepish.

Aaron unlocked the work truck and, dodging bags and piles of gear he had picked up that afternoon, slung her large duffle bag inside the crew cab. "Out with it."

She laughed. "Busted. You know me too well." Elle opened her passenger door and climbed in. Aaron navigated the behemoth of a work truck out of the narrow rows.

"You're right. He's more than just some guy. I was scared stupid on that flight and he helped calm me down."

Aaron nodded once, focusing on gliding the truck between two other, equally large work vehicles, both stopped in no-parking zones.

"I'd like to see him again." She added.

The air in the truck sparkled for an instant. He reached for the windshield wipers, then stopped, "Huh. Thought I just saw rain or something." He really didn't want to drive an hour in the rain on a crowded highway. Turning onto the road, he wondered if he should ask Elle to drive. First, he'd seen a man disappear, and then, phantom rain. Shaking his head, he turned off the highway they had just gotten on. "I need a coffee before we head out of town."

Chapter Five

Michael and Gaia were sitting together in one of Gaia's ethereal rose gardens.

"Oh stop it." Gaia kept her gaze focused on a particular rose bush. "She did technically ask to see him again."

Michael just continued to smile.

"I'm not breaking any of my own rules." Gaia scrunched her eyebrows together, almost distracted by the rose bush.

Still, Michael said nothing.

"Oh bother, I just want those two to be happy. You know I only provide doorways. It's up to them to walk through. Besides, Bodin really is a helicopter pilot. You know he's trained on every helicopter out there. It makes sense." Gaia nodded once toward the rose bush, then stood up, beaming like a particularly difficult puzzle was solved.

Michael looked from the rose bush, then back to Gaia, but said only, "Yeah, I know. You never give up on love for humans. Or cranky Changelings for that matter."

"Of course, I don't. You don't either. Now, he should be here any second." And with that, Bodin appeared before them.

****

"I need an extension," Bodin said without preamble, ignoring the beautiful, Divine garden and his manners.

"Hello to you, too," Gaia said warmly.

"I'm not kidding. I need an extension," he said again, this time crossing his arms across his chest in a defiant stance. He needed to stay focused and have a plan for why he should stay on the assignment. He wondered how he was going to defend the heavy petting and making out on airplanes. Damn it, he wanted—needed—to see Elle again.

"Of course you do, dear." Gaia ran her hands lovingly over vibrant leaves and petals.

"Stop being so damn agreeable and listen to me," Bodin snarled, slamming his hands on his hips in irritation, but was distracted by the shimmering foliage.

Gaia nodded at Michael, and Bodin was immediately suspicious of the smile the two shared. Michael stood and handed him an envelope. He took it cautiously and wondered what in the hell was going on.

"You will be her helicopter pilot for the next two weeks. All the paperwork and directions are in the envelope."

Bodin stared at the envelope in his hand and then at the serene Gaia.

"She's good, isn't she," Michael said, nodding his head toward Gaia.

"Yes, she is," Bodin answered, thinking of Elle.

"Go. Have a good time. I don't think I need to ask you to be nice this time." Gaia moved to smell a particularly radiant rose. "Oh, and Bodin...?"

Gaia's tone made him look up.

"Remember, discretion, please, the next time you decide to blink. There are eleven people in Alberta's Fort McMurray Airport wondering if they just hallucinated."

"They're fine," Bodin snapped, a bit bowled over at the opportunity he had been given and not caring a hoot if a few humans thought they were seeing things.

"Yes, of course, they're fine, but humans can be so fickle about the supernatural. The man who picked Elle up was one of those who saw you disappear. You will be his helicopter pilot for the next two weeks, as well."

Bodin groaned. Just what he didn't need, sissy humans getting in the way. He did need answers, though. "Michael, can I talk to you?"

"Sure."

"Anything I can help with?" Gaia had a hint of mischief to her tone.

"No," Bodin answered. "It's guy stuff."

Gaia smiled again, took out small shears, and clipped the delicate rose. "Give her this, too, please."

He took the lovely flower, a bit confused. Gaia had already turned her back and was tending the roses. She gave no explanation. He shrugged and said to Michael, "Come on," before stalking away.

The archangel easily caught up to his long strides. Bodin pretended that he did not notice Michael winking at Gaia. The two men walked a ways in silence. Michael strolled while Bodin wondered how in the hell he was supposed to ask what had happened on that plane.

"What the hell happened on that plane?" He demanded, getting hot again just thinking about it.

Michael glanced at Bodin as they walked. "I'll presume you are referring to your and Elle's…connection?"

"Hell yes, I'm talking about our connection, as you call it. What was that? How did that happen? What did I do, or she do? What's going on?"

"Relax. You clicked with someone, my guess, for the first time in your life. These things happen."

"What do you mean *clicked*? They don't just happen,

not to me, anyway," Bodin interrupted. "And she kissed me. Women don't just kiss me."

Michael laughed gently, and Bodin bellowed, "Don't patronize me. What happened?"

"Settle down. There are a few possibilities to explain what happened, but in this case, it is pretty straightforward. You two just click. You don't want to hear the rest."

"Yes, I do."

"No, you don't."

Bodin turned toward Michael. "Tell me, damn it."

Michael looked Bodin straight in the eye. "Love makes people click."

"What? That's ridiculous. And in any case, I just met her. How can love work like that?"

"Don't ask if you don't want to hear the answer."

Bodin started to retort, but thought better of it. He could be a pain in the ass, and he knew it. He had no idea why they had put up with him for this long.

"I really didn't try to do that…that thing."

"I know."

"I'm not sorry, but I didn't purposely go about that."

"I know."

Bodin exhaled. "What am I going to do?"

"You're going to be her pilot, for starters."

"I know, but I'm a Changeling. Isn't this wrong, or something?"

"Changeling as in still part human. Gaia made those parts, remember?"

Bodin was appalled to feel a blush creep up his cheeks. He didn't blush. "It's been a thousand years."

"I hear it's like riding a bike," Michael teased.

"It is not like riding a fucking bike," Bodin growled.

"I'm sure you'll do fine. She certainly wasn't

complaining on the plane."

Chapter Six

Elle had seen the sparkles, too. She didn't know why, but they reminded her of Bodin. She smiled to herself at the fanciful thought and took another sip of coffee. Bodin, who growled and frowned and sent images of mind-blowing sex and kissed her like she was Venus's long-lost sister, wasn't a sparkle kind of guy. She must be more tired than she thought, seeing random sparkles in work trucks. Or comparing herself to Venus.

Aaron and Elle drank their coffee in companionable silence for several miles, each lost in their own thoughts. The dashed yellow lines rolled by. The work camp they were driving to was about an hour north of Fort McMurray. The only sounds were the hum of tires against pavement and the SteelDrivers playing softly through the stereo speakers. The sun had set, and the night sky was an indigo blue. The first stars were just coming out. For once, the highway was blessedly sparse of cars and trucks. The Alberta Oil Sands were booming, and Highway 63, with its almost constant action, acted as a main artery. Quiet nights like this were scarce.

"We ran into a couple of bears last week," Aaron said, breaking the silence.

"I heard that." Elle remembered the e-mail that had gone out. She had known he was working in the area on a nearby lease.

"The first one we saw was fine. He just ran off as soon as he saw us. The other one, though, started stalking

Pete."

She whipped her head around. "Stalking? I didn't hear that part."

"Yeah. Freaked him out pretty good."

"I can imagine. I've seen several out in the bush, but I've never been stalked. I know it's possible, but thank god it is not typical bear behavior."

"I asked again about a bear monitor, but the client is hesitant to allow firearms on the lease, and there's no room in the budget."

Elle digested the information. Wildlife encounters were part of the job. They all had wilderness training and wildlife awareness training. They carried bear spray and bear bangers, but all the training and gadgets in the world were squat against an intent animal.

"There's no room in this project's budget for an increase in field crew, either," she said, knowing more people in a group could help dissuade an animal from investigating. "Guess we get to ride in each other's hip pockets on this one."

"Wear deodorant this time," Aaron joked.

Her mind switched from bears back to Bodin, and she smiled.

The two fell into a comfortable silence again. They both enjoyed the company and the quiet. Elle continued to think of Bodin. She was physically attracted to him, but something about him pulled her, and more than just him being gorgeous. It was kind of weird when she thought about it because he was quite gruff, had quite the bark to him. But she hoped she'd see him again. She wanted to know him. And who was she kidding? She wanted to check out those fascinating images they had shared, too. She hoped she would be given the chance and that she would be adventurous enough to take it. What had that been all about anyway? Who did that stuff happen to?

Apparently her, she thought wryly, taking a sip of coffee. Maybe she was turning over a new, wild, sex-goddess leaf. Yeah, right. She still wasn't sure what had happened. She fidgeted in her seat and wondered if she should confide in Aaron. He was so reasonable and understanding. He never judged her, either. Besides, she needed to tell someone before she exploded, she thought, and lifted the travel mug to her lips.

"Out with it."

Startled, Elle jumped and spilled a few drops of coffee. What was it with men being able to read her mind lately?

"Sorry, didn't mean to make you jump. But you've been sitting there fairly vibrating with something. Out with it. What's bugging you?"

She could trust Aaron, and she really would like to talk to someone about her experience. He might help make it seem more normal. "Remember that guy from the airport?"

"Yeah." Aaron kept his eyes on the road in front of them.

"Well, he helped me get through that turbulence all right, by…by…. Oh, this is so embarrassing. We had mental sex, all right!" she choked out.

"Like phone sex, but just talking in person?" He shot her a quick look.

"No. Like telepathically. Not talking, but getting the picture so much I actually came on the plane, right there sitting in my seat." She buried her face in her hands, mortified that she had confessed so much, even to Aaron.

"You actually climaxed? Without touching or

anything?" His tone mystified. "Huh."

"This isn't a science experiment, Aaron. I need that quicksilver mind to help me make sense of it now, not figure out future applications."

"What do you need? For me to say it didn't happen, or it did, or that it was all right, or that it was wrong? What do you need?" He asked, glancing over to give her a compassionate smile before focusing back on the road.

"I guess I need to know I am not crazy. And that I'm not a bad person for having mental sex with a complete stranger." Elle fidgeted and then added, "And then making out on the plane with said stranger." Hearing it, she couldn't even believe it herself, and she had been there!

"What?" In a more level tone he continued, "I mean, you did? Oh. Um, way to go, Elle?"

"Aaron!" She cried, horrified. "This is serious."

"I know it is. Sorry." He cleared his throat and snickered. "Geez, when you let your hair down, you really go for it. You aren't crazy. And you wouldn't be a bad person even if you had regular sex with a complete stranger. Cut yourself some slack. But, I have to ask about this guy. How did you end up having mental sex? And then making out? What did the guy do or say? Did he pressure you into this?"

She smiled at her best friend, touched by his concern. He would never say it, but she suspected that he knew how her self-esteem and self-worth had taken a beating under Jay's influence. She knew he still worried about her and would pound Jay to a pulp, too, if given the chance.

"No, he did not pressure me. I was freaking out at the turbulence. He started asking me mundane questions to get my mind off the bouncing plane, and then, the next thing I know, images of me and him in fabulous places and positions are flashing through my mind." She paused, remembering. "I had noticed him before. He's pretty hot, you know."

"Sure if you like the tall, dark, chiseled look," Aaron drawled. "But who likes that when they can have the short, stocky blond, like me?"

Elle laughed. "Who indeed?"

"Ouch."

"I'm just kidding, and you know it. You have a line-up of women, and we've already been around that block of why the two of us never hooked up."

"Darn chemistry. No offense, but kissing you would be akin to kissing my sister."

"Now whose turn is it to say ouch? Anyway, as I was saying about hot guy, yeah, fantastic images were racing through my mind, and they were so vivid, so real. I felt cherished, adored, almost worshiped, I guess. Put that all together and I came." She finished with a sigh. "His name is Bodin."

"You actually caught his name?"

"Yes, I caught his name!" She playfully punched him in the arm. "You're just mad I got to make-out with a hottie on the plane while you had to wait in all those lines picking up gear and supplies. Ha-ha." Fort McMurray had been a modest town that exploded with Oil Sands development. There were lines everywhere, and for everything, with retailers and the city unable to keep up with the booming demand.

A sour look came over Aaron's face. "Zip it. You owe me. I even found extra bear spray. Do you know how hard it is to find that in this town?"

"My hero," Elle cooed and batted her eyelashes.

Aaron rolled his eyes. "Save it for Bodin."

"I want you to meet him." She was serious, she trusted Aaron's uncanny judge of character. He had never liked Jay and had tactfully expressed his concern after she had introduced them. Deep down, she had known he was right, but she had just wanted him to be wrong. Sometimes, the idea of something beat the reality.

"I'm sure I will." He pulled off the highway into the work camp parking lot. He turned off the engine and turned toward Elle with gentle brown eyes. "I just want you to be happy."

"I know. And thanks." She leaned over and kissed him on the cheek. "I appreciate it."

"Good. Now, let's go eat supper, I'm starved." He rubbed his flat, six-pack belly.

Together, the two grabbed the baggage and gear and headed inside.

Chapter Seven

Michael answered Gaia's summons with speed. "Morning, Mum, what do you need?"

"Referee. Or a babysitter. Bodin's on his way to being an ass."

"He's always an ass."

"I know that. I just need you there. He could go in a few different directions, most of them not good. I'm hoping your presence will remind him to be an angel. He's quite taken with this woman. Actually, he feels lighter and better than he ever has, and the putz is completely avoiding thinking about why. But I digress." The Goddess held up her lovely hand, in emphasis. "His old warrior tendencies are simmering. She's completely safe. It's her best friend, Aaron, I'm worried about. He's a Diffuser and quite physical for this age, but he's no match against a cranky, seasoned warrior who just happens to be a Changeling, too."

"Still think you should put more boundaries on Changelings."

"I know. And I'm thinking about it. It's never been an issue with anyone except Bodin. He can be such a…a twerp."

"Putz? Twerp? He would be highly offended if he knew you called him that."

"Yes, well, I'm feeling bad that I called him an ass."

"I think he would appreciate ass more than putz or twerp." Michael laughed.

"Whatever. Just go remind him he's not a warrior anymore."

****

Elle woke up to the sound of her neighbor's alarm clock. Groggy and grumpy she cursed the paper-thin walls until she looked at her own watch and shrieked in alarm. "Shit! Shit! Shit!"

She had tossed and turned much of the night, thinking about Bodin, about her actions, worried she would never see him again and annoyed with herself for wanting to. Her inhibited side had scolded the fledgling Venus side until, amazingly, she had fallen into a deep, peaceful, rejuvenating sleep. She had been lucid, feeling calm and serene, and she could have sworn she had a plan. The *beep-beep-beep* had abruptly slammed her awake. In her haste, she had no idea what the plan was for as the feeling subsided.

She threw back the covers and jumped out of bed, berating herself for forgetting to set her own alarm. As she scurried about her room, her mind raced. He hadn't called. She had dreamed about him all night, and he hadn't called. The inhibited side of her won, and she decided yesterday was an anomaly for her rather ordered, mundane, definitely-not-a-sex-goddess life. Brushing her teeth, she muttered to herself around her toothbrush about alarms and men and turbulent flights. Not that she wasn't completely pissed he didn't call.

"Get a grip, so you made out and had mental sex with the guy. It's not like you'll ever see him again." She slammed her arms into her quick-dry shirt and yanked it over her head, muffling her muttering. "Or actually had sex with him. Guys don't actually call, how stupid to give him your number."

She continued to scold herself as her head popped out of the shirt and her gaze landed on her cell phone. She paused in her scrambling and picked up the phone. The display screen was dark. A huge smile spread across her face. The battery was dead. He might have tried to call. She might not be stupid for hoping he had. Elle reached to plug in her phone for later and almost tripped trying to pull on her field pants at the same time. She hopped to avoid crashing to the ground. They could use Aaron's phone in the field, if they needed it.

With renewed hope, she threw on the rest of her field clothes, and grabbed her pack of gear and paperwork before dashing out of her room. She was supposed to meet Aaron and the helicopter pilot at seven in the cafeteria. It was now ten after and she needed to grab breakfast, lunch for the road, or air so to speak, and coffee, definitely coffee. He might have called! She might not be stupid!

Elle flew into the cafeteria, skidded to a halt, and pulled up the shoulder of her zip-up fleece. She saw Aaron right away. He was sitting at a table with a man who had his back to her. Aaron noticed her coming toward them and started grinning like an idiot. She wondered what was wrong with him until the man sitting across from him turned around. Heat slammed into her and her heart started to pound in a furious staccato.

"Morning, Elle."

The simple greeting was the most intimate line in the world to her, she was stunned and deliriously happy. "Bodin!" She couldn't keep the delight from her tone. So much for playing it cool. Oh, who was she kidding? She was an open book. What was he doing here? Who cares, he was here!

She cheered to herself and soaked up the sight of him. He was hard and gorgeous and perfect. Elle looked down in alarm. Here she was, damn near panting, her hair still sleep tossed, in her rush. She hoped her clothes weren't on backward or something. Self-conscious, she tried to smooth her hair and pat her rumpled, luggage-wrinkled attire. She gave up almost immediately. She was wearing field clothes, for god sakes. Field clothes were never unwrinkled. Man, his lips were incredible.

"I didn't know you were going to be up here, too," She said with what she hoped was an easy tone.

"I tried calling you last night, but —"

"You did?" Elle interrupted, ecstatic. She wasn't stupid. *Shoot, too zealous! Be cool, be cool.*

"Yeah, but I just got your voice mail," Bodin answered, a bit hesitantly.

"My battery died." She was still reeling about a man having actually called after getting a number. Not only did he call, he didn't wait the three days or week or whatever was the game time for such things these days. She never remembered the rules her girlfriends told her about.

Aaron grinned. "Bodin's our helicopter pilot. Isn't that great?"

Elle turned from Aaron back to Bodin and, without thinking, said in dismay, "Fuck."

"What?" Bodin asked. Aaron gave her a puzzled look.

In a too-bright voice she answered, "I said, what luck!" How in the hell was she going to survive two weeks of helicopter survey with this guy? Passengers were not supposed to go licking their pilots midair, and she was going to have one hell of a time keeping her tongue and hands to herself.

She thought of all the remote landing sites she and Aaron had plotted the night before and groaned. This project was going to be a sheer test of will for her. All those wild, remote places, and Bodin there at every single one, waiting in a freaking helicopter. Talk about fantasy come to life. She couldn't sleep with her helicopter pilot. It was unethical, right? Unprofessional, for sure. Likely a big fat no-no in some handbook, somewhere. Holy crap, why was he so gorgeous? He was wearing ordinary work clothes for the area: pullover, field pants, and scuffed hiking boots. But on him, they dripped hot.

"Elle. Elle? Yoo-hoo, Elle!"

"Hmm?" She couldn't stop staring. Bodin was gazing right back at her. It was taking all her concentration to remember she was technically at work. Aaron had finally taken pity on her and was trying to steer the ogling and conversation back to work.

"I was just giving Bodin the coordinates for today while we waited for you. Why don't you grab breakfast so we can go over the maps and you can eat at the same time?"

Grateful, she looked at Aaron. "Breakfast, good idea. Be right back."

She walked away and silently berated herself. She had to pull it together. Women worked with men who dripped with sensuality all the time. She could learn to deal with it. Focus, she had to focus. Pant…lick…caress…*stop it, stop it, stop it. Focus!* She continued the scolding while she grabbed a muffin, a banana, and a coffee from the food counter.

****

Aaron watched Elle walk away from their table before he turned and stared Bodin straight in the eye. "So far, I like you, but hurt her and I'll saw your balls off with this spoon." Aaron picked up the rather ordinary-looking spoon he had used to stir his coffee and pointed it at Bodin.

Bodin had been replaying Elle's words. He had been surprised and relieved that she sounded so excited. He hadn't dated anyone, ever. People didn't date a thousand years ago, not like today, anyway. He had no idea how to do it.

Now he glared at Aaron when what he really wanted to do was punch him in the face. No one had ever spoken to him like that. Ever. His glare and reputation had always dissuaded anyone from the sort. He had killed for lesser transgressions back in his day. In hindsight, that had been rather over the top. A lot could happen in a thousand years, though, and did. That whole angel thing had seriously curbed his penchant for violent solutions. Before Bodin could answer, Elle was walking back to the table with her small breakfast.

****

Aaron saw Elle's meager plate. "What's with the bird breakfast?"

She shrugged and countered, "I'll pack a good lunch." She had heard what Aaron had said to Bodin, and although she was touched, she didn't want anything to escalate. If looks could kill, Aaron would be dead a hundred times over by the way Bodin was glaring at him. She needed to diffuse the situation, pronto. Stupid men and their posturing, she thought. Like a bunch of peacocks with their feathers all ruffled. Well, she had the cock part right, anyway.

Bodin was about to erupt. "Okay guys, let's check out those maps." She forced the two bulldogs to pay attention while she went over the list of high-potential areas they were to cover in relation to the topographic maps and possible helicopter landing sites. Twenty minutes later, they had settled down for the most part and actively engaged in the day's planning, with only a few sideways glares at each other. Elle wondered if there was a reference guide to male non-verbal communication. She felt she had missed an entire silent conversation.

"Now, are you two done grunting and beating your chests?"

Aaron grinned sheepishly and winked at her before glancing at Bodin. "For now."

Bodin gave a curt nod, but kept scowling.

"Good. I'm trusting you," she said, nodding at Bodin, "to get us around safely and not leave us out there in the hopes Aaron will have time to think about not being a jerk next time. And I need you"—she nodded at Aaron—"to help me find any sites out there, not get mauled by a bear, and to not irritate the piss out of our pilot." She stared at one man, then the next. "Understand?"

"Yes, ma'am," the men said in unison before looking at each other, startled.

"See? You guys are getting along already. We might even be able to have beers together before this project is done."

The small group rose from the table. Aaron grabbed his coffee spoon, pointed it once at Bodin, and gave him a determined frown before pocketing it.

Elle wondered if shock collars should have been on

her packing list.

****

Michael had taken a seat at a nearby table and inconspicuously watched the little drama unfold. He had to hand it to Elle. She had reined in the two hardheaded males and had them almost liking each other at the end. He stood and walked over as they were about to leave.

"I didn't hit anybody," Bodin whispered in greeting, but his face was a study in irritation.

"Yet," Michael retorted. He kept his voice as quiet as Bodin had.

"Hi," Elle said, curious. She had collected the maps and notes, and they were now balanced precariously under one arm as she grabbed for her kit bag with the other.

Bodin scowled and glared at the newcomer before saying, "Elle, Aaron, meet Michael. My boss and brother."

Chapter Eight

"What was your brother doing here?" Elle asked Bodin as they were headed to the helicopter with Aaron after Michael's departure.

Bodin caught Aaron glancing over, as if curious about his response. "My guess is he is checking up on me. I'm not exactly cordial. He probably wants to make sure I don't punch the client or something."

With that, he threw Aaron another glare, who only laughed in amusement. The last twenty minutes had cooled Bodin down for the most part, but he still did not like how comfortable the pair were or that Aaron knew what Elle often had for breakfast. He had never experienced jealousy before. No woman had ever captured his attention enough for him to care if someone else wanted her or even had her. Never bothered him before, but the thought of Aaron and Elle together, ever, had put him on a hair-trigger temper.

Aaron had a quick mind and was quite amusing. Bodin might even come to like the guy if there was nothing going on between him and Elle. Giving himself a mental kick in the pants, he reminded himself that he didn't like people and that he was only here for the assignment. And to hopefully get laid for the first time in centuries. Bodin thought of the slang phrase. Each time had its own colorful and crass descriptions of sex.

Frowning, he wondered when Michael would put in another appearance. No doubt he was updating Gaia this very moment. He hated being checked up on.

Elle had been quiet too long. Nodding toward the helicopter, he asked, "You going to be okay?"

Her face scrunched in confusion for a heartbeat before she broke into a wide grin. "Oh, I love helicopters. It's just planes that freak me out."

"That doesn't make any sense." If Elle wasn't afraid of flying in helicopters, what was he doing here? He would be pulled off the assignment.

"It's a fear. Who said anything about it being rational?" She countered, skipping a step and kicking a pebble. "You're just mad you won't have to take my mind off flying."

"Yes, of course that's it." Just to see her reaction, he added, "I just might, though."

A bright flush colored her cheeks, and she stumbled.

Aaron rolled his eyes good-naturedly. "Can you at least turn off my headset if you do?"

Elle turned to him. "Sorry, sorry. I should shut up. We're at work."

"Not on my account. The longer we're up here, though, I retain the right to change my mind." Aaron shifted the shovels he was carrying.

The smile Aaron flashed at Elle had Bodin frowning and wondering how to talk Gaia into letting him stay.

****

The small group was efficient going through its preflight tasks and was airborne in no time. Elle sat up front. She tried to focus on the sweeping landscape below them, but she found herself noticing Bodin's competent hands working the controls and his muscular thighs mere inches from her. It felt good to be interested in somebody again, made her feel alive again. She had dated Jay for only a few months, but she was still putting herself back together from the experience. She hadn't liked the person she had become with him—withdrawn, miserable, and lonely. She had neglected her friends because Jay hadn't liked them and hadn't wanted her hanging out with them. She had gone along with him because it felt good to be wanted by someone.

Elle realized now that she had not even really liked him. She'd just liked the idea of him. They had met when her parents had been going through a particularly rough patch. He had taken her mind off their looming divorce. She was grateful she had come to her senses when she did, although she still kicked herself for even getting involved with him in the first place. Aaron and some of her other good friends reminded her to give herself a break. Everyone makes bonehead decisions at one time or another. She wished hers could have been a bad haircut instead.

Elle was quiet while she thought about Bodin and his boss. There was something about his boss that she couldn't put her finger on it. He was nice enough and didn't say or do anything out of the ordinary, but she felt different the moment she saw him. Safe. Not that she had been feeling particularly unsafe before, but she had felt soothed somehow around him. How weird. She had never been tuned into her feelings like she had been yesterday and today.

It took a while to get to the project area, and she finally made herself focus on work instead of Bodin. She gazed out at the landscape before them. They were following the Athabasca River north. Elle's trained eye caught everything now that she was focused. A moose and calf started trotting along the shoreline. She pointed and

smiled. She loved this part of the job. They had left the
congestion farther south, and the leases they were flying
over were still quite wild, for now.

When they approached the project area, they did a
cursory flyover, and Elle and Aaron jotted a few notes. The
flyover helped them get a feel of the overall project area.
They also had to find suitable landing sites to meet up with
Bodin before they started their hopscotching of high-
potential areas. Bodin would drop Elle and Aaron off and
fly to the next pick-up spot while the two conducted their
archaeological survey, making their way to where the
helicopter waited for them. Then they would fly to the next
target area and do the same thing. The remote work called
for extra gear as a safety precaution, and Aaron and Elle
shared the load equally. They each also had their regular
work gear. Everything condensed down to fit in a medium-
sized backpack, except the shovels used for test pitting.

Bodin found a small clearing near Elle and Aaron's
starting point and landed in the tight space with expert ease.
It was clear he was very good at his job. Few pilots would
have tried landing where he did. Elle glanced out the
window at what passed for ground in the muskeg, then took
one last look at her dry work boots, and tried to commit the
feeling to memory. In a few seconds, her boots and lower
legs would be soaked.

Bodin cautiously lowered the helicopter toward the
ground and said into the headset, "Careful, it's going to be
a soft landing." Elle and Aaron both acknowledged they
had heard. A few moments later Bodin's voice came over
the headset again, "Ok, you guys are good to go."

Elle and Aaron unclipped out of their belts. Both had
flown enough for it to be second nature to clip the belts
back together behind them. Pilots really hated a loose

seatbelt flapping. She had been on the job with a couple of rookies who forgot. One of their seat belts had gotten slammed in the door and flapped on the outside of the helicopter until the pilot noticed and had to land to correct the costly mistake. Paint jobs on helicopters were not cheap. Neither was dinged metal.

"See you in about an hour and a half," Elle said before taking off her headset.

Bodin nodded curtly. She didn't take offense. She knew he was concentrating on keeping the helicopter steady at the soft landing. The ground was muskeg and would not support the weight of the large machine. He kept the helicopter hovering next to the liquid ground as Aaron and Elle jumped out. They moved with practiced efficiency, grabbing their gear from the external side compartment and staying low to clear the danger zone of the rotating blades and whipping wind and debris the blades had kicked up. They crouched a distance away and watched as the helicopter lifted off, cleared the trees, and roared away.

****

"I've never flown with any other pilot who would have landed here," Aaron admitted, his voice holding a touch of awe, as they watched the helicopter disappear.

"He's good." Elle stood and slung on her pack. "And he shaved a thirty-minute hike off our start by getting us this close instead of the other landing site."

"Not bad," Aaron said, shouldering his own pack and grabbing for his shovel. "Not bad at all. The other spot was likely wetter, too. Although any kind of wet boots first thing in the morning sucks."

Elle agreed. Her shoulders sank a little when she saw

her work boots. She and Aaron had crouched on the higher ground of trees ringing the muskeg landing site when Bodin took off, and water was squishing out of her boots when she transferred her weight. Feeling clammy, wet boots was one thing, seeing water bead out of them definitely made it worse. *Oh the joys of field work,* she thought to herself, snickering.

"Remember that Striped Tree Site?" They had been dropped at a site where the water went well above their knees.

"How could I forget?" Aaron muttered.

He had been walking point and had fallen face first into the water, tripping on deadfall that had been covered by overgrown grass and water. They looked at each other and burst out laughing.

****

The day flew by. The late fall weather was cold enough to have gotten rid of the bugs, but still comfortable. If they had had dry boots, it would have been ideal. The two had worked together so long that they immediately fell into a comfortable rhythm.

They stopped to have a late lunch with Bodin at the second rendezvous site. Elle plopped down on the grass and undergrowth and immediately unlaced her boots. She pulled the still-wet footwear off with two great heaves, opened up the laces as far as they would go, and pointed the openings into the direction of the light breeze. She glanced up to see Bodin, who was watching her with a questioning smile, and wondered if she was too comfortable with him. Her mom would freak if she knew her daughter had taken off her work boots in front of coworkers. She smiled to herself. Her mom would hyperventilate if she knew what Elle had done on the plane.

"What?" She laughed as she pulled off her soaked socks and wiggled her pruned toes in the wind and teased, "Is it my feet? They can't smell that bad; they're too cold."

"I'm going to go check out that ridge," Aaron said abruptly, getting up and grabbing his lunch and kit bag. "Call me when you guys want to leave." He walked off without a backward glance.

Elle watched Aaron retreat and knew he was giving her and Bodin time alone. She was grateful for his insight and understanding, but suddenly nervous. She wasn't afraid of Bodin; she was afraid of herself and what she wanted.

"Guess it was your feet," Bodin joked, as he walked over.

The words sounded stiff to her. She doubted he often tried for humor.

His hesitation was palpable, before he asked a bit gruffly, "Cold feet?"

Elle glanced at her goose bumps and tried not to wince at Bodin's tone. "In more ways than one," she admitted, ducking her head. She was not sophisticated or coy. She was nervous with what had already happened and what she wanted to have happen. She was seriously into him and that scared her. She had blown it with her last taste in men. No, that was an excuse. Jay was a moron, and she had never allowed him to get close to her. She was more connected to Bodin than she had ever been with anyone, even Aaron. They had connected on a level that seemed to transcend reality. And she had met him eighteen hours ago!

"Please don't be scared of me," he whispered, misreading her shyness.

"I'm not scared of you. I'm scared of myself." She

met his eyes before darting her gaze down again.

"Relax," he commanded softly. "We're still on the clock. I'm going to warm your feet. That's it. Perfectly reasonable and respectable."

She gave a helpless laugh. Everything was in overdrive. Relaxing would be great, if she had any idea how to tone down her senses around him. He sat down where she was wiggling in the wind. He took one foot, placed it on his lap, and just held it between his big hands.

When they were feeling all toasty, he started massaging them. She had never had a foot massage in her life and was surprised feet could be such an erogenous zone. As he worked his warm hands over her heating skin, Elle started to relax. She lay down and rested her head on her pack, her foot in his lap. There was no noise except the slight wind through the trees and a sigh or two escaping her lips.

"Why archaeology?" Bodin asked after a while.

"I don't know why, but I love the past. I love the connection to the past an artifact or landscape gives. It feels like sharing something with a complete stranger of a different time, but knowing we really are the same. People are people. I could sit down with whoever made that scraper we found this morning and talk about their kids or how lucky we are the weather is holding out or laugh about the antics of a whiskey jack stealing food."

Elle saw the moon, a subtle crescent in the pale blue sky. "I love it when the moon is out. I sometimes see the moon and think about all the people, throughout all the ages, who have gazed up at that same moon."

She looked at him a moment before shifting her attention skyward again. "I don't know. It just helps me feel connected to humanity. It's no wonder why some cultures revere the moon. She is magical."

The two sat in comfortable silence, staring at the moon.

****

After a while, Bodin turned to Elle and said, "You're quite a woman." She floored him. She knew instinctually what a lot of people couldn't grasp after being told or shown. He also had never met anyone who was so thoughtful or caring. She seemed to love all around her. She gave her love freely, whether a smile to a flight attendant when she was scared shitless or teasing a laugh out of a grump like him. Her career choice even linked the past and present. She brought people together just by being herself; he had a knack for driving people away. Bodin was still a bit in awe that she was still here paying attention to him. She was a million times too good for him. Lucky for him, he didn't care. If she'd have him, he was hers.

"What about you?"

"What do you want to know?" Bodin picked up her other foot.

"Everything."

Alarm slammed through him. She laughed. "Okay, we'll start with why a helicopter pilot?"

Bodin relaxed. He could handle that question. "I've always been fascinated with flight. When the opportunity arose, I decided to take it." He didn't mention the opportunity had occurred when he was nine hundred and fifty-four years old. Or that it was on an assignment in the training and he decided to continue with it after the assignment was finished. He wanted to tell her everything. He didn't want any secrets between them, but he knew that wasn't possible. Frickin' Angel Code crap.

"Oh yeah, I meant to ask you before, what did you mean on the plane when you said it was scheduled turbulence of a sort?" Elle had resumed her sky gazing, chewing on a piece of grass, seemingly oblivious to his discomfort.

Out of habit, he groaned. Of course, she had a good memory. He had known it was dicey telling her the cryptic comment on the plane, and not just because it was privileged information. Few things captured his attention, but he was utterly fascinated with flight. He had never shared any part of himself while on assignment. He realized, though, that he wanted to share this with her.

"Would you believe me if I said all the Elements were more real and active than people give them credit for? The people who invented flight were actually visited by Air in a dream, did you know that?" Bodin asked, excited.

"You're funny. I like your sense of humor."

Bodin saw she didn't believe him and couldn't blame her. He was a bit relieved, actually. The desire to share himself with her was a new feeling, and he needed a breaking-in period. Instead of elaborating and setting her straight, he said, "Could I tell you the answer later?" He willed her to give him time.

"Of course." Her tone was light but her eyes curious. "We better eat before Aaron gets back. I can't survey without food. I can't watch TV without food," Elle amended, then shot her head up, alarmed.

Bodin saw fear cross her face. He was instantly on guard and took a quick look around for danger. "What is it? What's wrong?"

She took his hands and hauled herself to a seating position. "Nothing. Not anymore and not ever again," she said with determination.

"Try again. You were just scared. I want to know why."

She hesitated before shrugging. "Jay, my ex-boyfriend, used to be on my case about dieting. He told me he didn't care if I was anorexic or bulimic. He wanted me skinny and didn't care how I got there." She was clearly embarrassed at the admission.

"You're perfect. You're healthy and you're beautiful. Jay's an idiot." Bodin hid his fury that her words invoked. Jay would be eating through a straw if Bodin got his hands on him. Screw the Angel Code. Some guys just needed their asses kicked into next week.

She leaned over and kissed him, interrupting his thoughts of retribution.

Bodin sat up, a bit stunned. "What was that for?" Women didn't just kiss him. At least, they never had in the past.

Elle's smile lit up her face. "For being you. Come on, let's eat."

And that was that. It was so honest and straightforward. He wasn't used to that. She kept surprising him.

The two ate their lunches, sneaked caresses, and just enjoyed each other's company. Neither wanted the time to end, but each knew they had to get a move on.

Aaron strolled up when they had just finished packing up.

"Good timing." Elle reached to put her wet boots back on. "I was just about to call out to you."

"Yeah, right." Aaron leaned against his shovel and snickered good-naturedly. "The sooner we finish today, the sooner you two can *talk* at camp."

Elle tied her laces and stood, brushing off her backside. "Good point. Let's go." She looked over at Bodin and wiggled her eyebrows.

He winked at her, then went back to his usual state of glowering for Aaron's benefit. He saw Elle roll her eyes. "You're such a faker," she said in a conspiratorial whisper. "I know you're really a sweetheart."

Sweetheart? Now he was a *sweetheart?* As bizarre as it sounded to him, if it was an endearment from Elle, he'd take it.

Chapter Nine

Aaron shut off the shower taps and snapped the towel off the hook. Drying himself off, he thought of the day and his mind wandered to Bodin. It was just weird being around the guy. Grabbing his jeans, Aaron crammed his muscular legs into the sturdy material and yanked on the zipper. He was ecstatic Elle was so happy, but he still didn't trust Bodin and didn't know if he even liked the guy or not.

Okay, that wasn't entirely fair, or true. He pulled a dark green T-shirt over his head with more vigor than required and stewed. He was a guy, and he knew how guys thought and what they thought of. It was pretty obvious that Bodin wanted to fuck Elle eighteen ways before nightfall, and then another thirty-four before morning. The thought made Aaron want to throw Bodin across the cafeteria they were supposed to meet at for supper, and then beat him with the industrial coffeepot that made such shitty coffee. It had nothing to do with liking the guy or not.

He was pissed off and knew it wasn't reasonable. Still, he always had felt protective of Elle, like an older brother or something. Foregoing a comb, he ran his fingers through his wet hair. Thank god he didn't feel more than brotherly for Elle. Watching the two together would make him puke. He had heard of people falling for each other at first sight, but he'd thought that was just girls talking after they had sex with guys they'd just met, to make themselves feel better. Most women he knew thought casual sex was a bad thing and reasoned away their actions with weird ideas of love or booze or rebound. Or, like Elle, just felt really guilty.

Why couldn't they just accept it for what it was, sex between strangers that sometimes went somewhere and sometimes didn't? Elle had told him he was too insensitive, that it was different for women. She had been so upset with what she had done with Bodin on that airplane. They both clearly were into each other. Out of habit, he slapped on his watch and grabbed his cell phone. He didn't understand the problem. Or maybe didn't understand the emotional or mental baggage women went through. Did he just think that? Jesus, he had to start hanging out with more men. Elle was turning him a bit too sensitive. Maybe Bodin wouldn't be that bad, after all. Aaron jammed his feet into a pair of flip flops and stormed out of his room to the cafeteria.

****

Bodin walked into the cafeteria looking for Elle. They had made plans to meet for supper and then play foosball in the lounge. He hoped that was code for dumping Aaron, going to one of their rooms, and having lots and lots of loud sex. Okay, so the loud was negotiable, but he wasn't budging on the hope for lots of it. He spotted Aaron. Bodin grabbed food and, sitting down across from Elle's best friend, wondered where the hell she was. He didn't want to talk to Aaron. Well, to be honest, he actually was starting to like the guy. But like his relationship with Michael, he didn't want to admit it. Ruined his complete asshole facade.

Aaron nodded in greeting and continued eating. The two men sat in silence a while before Aaron asked, "Are you into hockey?"

Bodin shook his head, pretty sure he knew where this was going.

"Football? Lacrosse? Rugby?"

Bodin had read most of the energy Aaron had been vibrating with. The guy needed a dose of testosterone. Poor guy. His best friend was a woman, albeit a very cool woman, but a female all the same. He had the insane urge to make the guy feel better. Acknowledging the slip in his anti-people armor, he shrugged and answered anyway. "Most martial arts. I caught an Australian rules football game a while back. Now that's a game I could get into." Bodin took a bite of his steak. He liked sports where the point was to beat the piss out of the opponent. Peering closer at Aaron, he thought the man might want to pound the piss out of him.

Aaron's face lit up. He'd opened his mouth as if to answer Bodin, when Elle walked up and said, "Not a chance, Aaron."

"What?" Aaron asked, going for sheepish and failing miserably.

"You know what. You guys are not fighting. End of story." She sat down and stabbed her baked potato with her fork.

Bodin looked from Elle to Aaron, interested.

She swung her gaze to him. "I said not a chance, and I meant it. You guys have been playing nice, so far, and it better stay that way."

"It would just be a little sparring, no big deal."

"Yeah right. You don't know how to *just spar,* and I doubt Bodin does either."

"Elle." Aaron's voice had the barest hint of a whine.

"Stacy." Elle said the name with finality.

Aaron appeared to be pouting. "Sure, bring her into

it.”

Elle smiled and said sweetly, “Sometimes I can't play nice with you,” before popping a small bite of baked potato into her mouth.

Bodin looked at the two friends. “Who's Stacy?” He was trying not to stare at the corner of Elle's lips, but a dab of sour cream was playing havoc with his good intentions.

He watched as she licked the corner of her lips before saying, “This incredibly gorgeous woman Aaron has been hot over for about, oh, two years now. It's really the only dirt I have on Aaron and it's not really dirt at all.”

“What's the big deal?” Bodin was trying to focus on the conversation instead of Elle's lips.

“She's my advisor's daughter,” Aaron answered glumly, picking at his food.

“Haven't you graduated already?”

“Yes. But, there's more, and it's complicated. Elle, threat worked, can we drop it?” Aaron asked, irritated. “Threaten Bodin with something.”

“No head for you.” Elle's voice was cheerful as she swung her gaze back to him.

Bodin's other head, the one on top of his neck, whipped around in surprise. “That's a possibility?” he asked her, before turning to glare at Aaron. “You're going to pay for that.”

Aaron laughed at Elle. “See, you started a fight anyway. As soon as your back is turned, Bodin's going to try and kick my ass.”

“I *am* going to kick your ass,” Bodin growled.

“Boys.” Still laughing, she held up her hand. “How about I just say please? Aaron, I won't tell Stacy anything. Bodin, well, we'll continue this later,” she said, blushing profusely.

"Elle," Bodin said in warning. He knew between the conversation, the blush, and the curious expression on her face, everything she was thinking about. His dick was hard now in anticipation of her beautiful mouth wrapped around him.

She stared at him, startled, and then smiled. He nearly jumped out of his chair. Bodin wanted to throw her over his shoulder and carry her off to his room.

Heat was coursing through Bodin's body, but the fire in Elle's eyes scorched him in all the right places. They both were coiled, spring-ready. The energy vibrated between them. He had never experienced anything like it. He could actually see their energies swirling together. Either had only to say the word and they both would sprint to the closest room.

"For the love of god, you two, go! You're getting me turned on and I'm going 'home' with myself tonight. And it's kind of creeping me out." Aaron waved his hand toward the door.

Bodin was trying to remember to breath. Elle's chest was rising and falling at a rapid pace.

"Seriously, go!" Aaron sounded almost frantic. "I feel like a voyeur just sitting here with you two. Go!" This time, Aaron pointed at the door in emphasis.

Elle's face lit up even more, her clear blue eyes dancing, and she said to Bodin, "Race you!" and sprinted out of her chair.

Bodin looked at Aaron and said, "Thank you." Then he tore after her.

****

Aaron stared at the doorway Elle and Bodin had

disappeared through, the sound of their laughing fading. He shook his head to clear the image and picked up his fork. Their sexual energy had been potent and tangible. Aaron felt uncomfortable he had picked up such intimate energy between his best friend and her new boyfriend. It was pure, though, and honest. That helped. If someone was going to screw his best friend's brains out, Aaron couldn't ask for a better energy source.

He had never seen sexual energy like that. It was beautiful, intense, almost divine in its purity. No wonder Elle had made out with Bodin on the plane and had mental sex or whatever that was. Aaron felt like he just saw God, or something. He didn't know if he should be concerned or consider it an epiphany.

****

Bodin easily caught up with Elle and started nuzzling her neck. Laughing, she said, "Not in the hall. I have to see these guys all season."

A man walked by them, then, and whistled with a knowing grin.

"Good point." Bodin wanted to smack the guy, but he wanted to get Elle in her room more. They reached her door, and she fumbled with the key. He wound up to ram the door with his shoulder, and playful panic crossed her face.

"Bodin." She held out her hand and wiggled her room key. "How 'bout we try this, instead? I want to close that door after we're inside."

Another good point. Elle managed to unlock and open the door on the second try. She made it three steps into the small room before he turned her, swallowed her up in his arms, and kicked the door closed behind them. His lips crashed against hers, and she ground against him everywhere: lips, chest, arms, hips, legs. The intensity of the kiss rocked both of them, and Bodin started to teeter. Her weight shifted on the kiss and they both tumbled to the floor, knocking over extra gear and nearly tipping the small wastebasket. He had tried to turn to buffer her when a distant part of his brain registered what was happening.

She landed on top of him. If she noticed they had fallen, she gave no indication. The kiss had never stopped.

She worked the snaps on his denim shirt, while her lips found his neck. Bodin groaned at the feel of her soft lips against the pulse at his throat. He managed to grab the bottom hem of her shirt and yanked it up.

He pulled her shirt roughly over her head, and she made a noise that sounded like a purr. He wanted her naked, *now.* By her frantic movements, she wanted the same thing. She grabbed both sides of his shirt, snapped the rest of it open, and exposed the broad expanse of his torso. Her face shone with delight and appreciation.

Elle lowered her head to his chest and stroked her cheek against his hair, seemingly oblivious to his squirming arms tangled in the shirt. The feel of her soft cheek against his skin undid his good intensions. He gave his shirt a couple of well-placed tugs and heard the rip of fabric, before he sent it sailing across the room. She reached behind her and unhooked her bra, her eyes never leaving Bodin's. He grabbed the straps on her shoulders and teased them down. His green eyes took in the seductive sight of her breasts.

Bodin had dreamed of putting his face between them, and he did so now. He inhaled the warm scent of her. He never wanted to let go. Elle started kissing him again and, burrowing against his chest, kissed lower and lower. She kissed her way down his treasure trail, the trail of hair leading below his belt. Bodin thought he would explode right then. She hadn't even gotten in his pants, and he was rock hard and more than ready to go. He didn't know if he could last her wrapping her sexy lips around his penis. Grabbing her torso, he hefted her back up him. "Kiss me there and round one is over." He panted.

She squirmed against him, once, and Bodin sucked in a breath. Her eyes went wide before understanding hit her. Her tempting lips spread into a brilliant smile and she slid off him, shimmying out of her jeans and her panties.

Bodin groaned in satisfaction and nearly jumped out of his trousers. He kissed his way up her bare leg and let his hands roam her. His lips pressed against where she was hottest. Elle was more than ready for him, but he had to be certain. He needed her to be having as much fun as he was. He slid one finger inside her while his tongue stroked her clitoris. He worked his finger in and out a few times before slowly fitting a second of his long fingers inside her. He watched her face a moment, still licking her. Her expression was one of rapture and she pushed her hips against his face. He looked down, and again fit his fingers inside her, stretching her, while his tongue and lips continued to work her.

Elle's hips bucked, and Bodin withdrew his fingers to tease and circle her. She started clawing at him, trying to drag him up her. There was no mistaking her desire. She wanted him, in her, *now.*

A distant part of Bodin's mind remembered the small package Michael had given him. Some things about sex had changed in the last thousand years. Where the hell were the condoms? Jeans pocket. He had to get to his jeans pocket.

Groping with one hand while keeping his face still between Elle's legs, he grabbed his jeans and found the handful of condoms. He had been optimistic earlier, thank god. Pulling one out, he straightened enough to put it on before lowering himself on top of Elle.

She cooed when he gently lowered his weight against her and his hips pressed hers into the carpet. Elle pulled him toward her as he positioned himself. Bodin looked at her, memorizing this moment, her face flushed and radiant. A tenderness swept over him, and he slowly entered her. The soft emotion was soon replaced with driving hunger.

Testing her readiness, he stroked cautiously a few times. As hot as he was, he didn't want to hurt her. But she eagerly met him, and he increased his pace. Elle matched him stroke for stroke, squeezing him with each thrust. Bodin watched her climax build and build. He could feel how close she was.

He was breathing hard, both from exertion and trying to hold back as long as he could. He saw the moment Elle's wave broke as she spasmed with the ripples of release. His own was right there and with one final thrust, he roared with his pulsing release.

****

Bodin gently kissed Elle's lips, her cheeks, her forehead. His smile was so warm that she knew she had melted. He kissed her on the nose, before leaning over to discard the used condom in the still-upright wastebasket. She savored the sight of him and remembered the tenderness that had come over his handsome face right before he entered her. It shook her. *It would be so easy to fall for him.* The thought didn't scare her, and that terrified her. She'd worry about it later. For now, she just wanted the moment and Bodin. "Next time I'm on top." She laughed, pulling at the boot that was lodged behind her head. "So that was what my head was slamming into."

Bodin grabbed the boot out of her hand and tossed it across the room. "Sorry," he murmured before lowering his head and sizzling her with a kiss.

Eager, Elle met his lips and returned the passionate embrace, heat kindling again. Suddenly he released her lips and pulled them both up, sweeping her into his arms before tumbling them onto the bed.

"I really meant to make it to the bed. I'll make it up to you." Bodin's smile was wolfish. He took his time admiring her flushed, naked body laid out before him.

Elle looked right back. "Promises, promises. I still want you"—she pointedly glanced at his suddenly rising flesh—"in my mouth."

Bodin's eyes blazed. "You want to be on top and have me in your mouth?" He stroked the inside of her thigh. "Sounds interesting."

Elle shivered and nodded, loving the sight of his magnificent body. Seductively, she slid down and started kissing Bodin's chest, loving the feel of his hair tickling her. She worked her way down, trailing kisses along his ribs and flat belly. She loved the feel of his strong body. When her lips moved over the head of his penis and she darted out her tongue, she heard his groan in pleasure. Elle amended her earlier thought—she had fallen for him.

Chapter Ten

Morning came entirely too early as far as Elle was concerned. The alarm on her watch beeped from the desk, and she desperately wanted to throw a pillow at it. Knowing the blasted thing would shut off by itself soon, she snuggled into Bodin's embrace instead.

"Morning," Bodin murmured and kissed the top of her head.

She tightened her arms around his warm body. "Five more minutes." Her words were muffled against the side of his chest.

"We've already reset the alarm twice," Bodin said, stroking her shoulder.

"Can't it be a rainy day?" Elle grumbled, wiping a wisp of hair out of her sleepy eyes. She was exhausted. They had kept each other up most of the night. Between the sex and just talking, they had finally fallen asleep an hour before dawn. She wasn't used to a few hours' sleep, let alone sex marathons.

He tilted her chin up and gave her a strong kiss. "Let's go. The sooner we get out there, the sooner we finish and can get back in bed."

Elle kissed him back. "Oh, all right, you rational man." She grabbed a pillow as she got up from bed and hit him on the head with it. Bodin reached out his long arms and caught her around the waist, hauling her back in bed and into his embrace. His hand hit a ticklish spot, and she erupted into uncontrollable laughter.

"Stop. Stop," Elle sputtered, trying to catch her breath in between fits of laughter.

"Soon." Bodin laughed, still tickling her.

She felt his chest vibrate, and the sweetest sound Elle had ever heard rumbled out of him. Bodin had stopped tickling her and was just laughing. She gave him a spontaneous hug. "Keep doing that. Keep laughing. I love that sound."

Bodin wrapped his arms around her and hugged her back. "Keep giving me something to laugh about," he said earnestly.

Elle gave Bodin another squeeze and opened her eyes. She caught sight of the watch face sitting harmlessly on the desk and exclaimed, "Shit, shit, shit! We're so late!" With a giggle, she wiggled out of Bodin's embrace and started grabbing her field clothes. "Aaron is so going to tease me!" She grabbed her kit bag. Bodin stood and got dressed.

"You're cute when you're all frazzled," he said, zipping his pants.

Elle tried not to pay attention to what was in Bodin's pants. "This isn't funny! Okay it is, but only because it's Aaron. Thank god he's the one I'm working with on this project." She did a quick scan of her room, hoped she wasn't forgetting anything important, and pulled Bodin out the door.

****

Aaron smiled when Elle and Bodin walked into the cafeteria. Well, Elle walked. Bodin sauntered. "Hey, you two crazy kids," Aaron said in greeting. "I'm sorry, were we supposed to meet at eight? Because I thought seven, but it's closer to eight now." Aaron took a sip of coffee, almost hiding another smile.

Elle gave him a mock grumpy face before dissolving into laughter. "Busted," she said and grabbed for the scone on his plate.

"Hey!" He swiped the plate out of her reach. "Get your own high carb, refined sugar, empty calorie treat."

Bodin deftly snatched the pastry and took a big bite. Aaron nodded at Bodin. "I'm going to let you have that, but only because you're bigger. And because Elle has a definite twinkle in her eye this morning."

"Aaron!" Elle sputtered.

"It's true. Enjoy it. I've grabbed you guys bag lunches already. I figured you might be a bit late getting ready this morning," he was unable to keep the snicker out of his voice. "We've got a lot of areas to hit today, though, so let's get a move on."

****

They were airborne and on their way several minutes later. Aaron watched Elle down her travel mug of coffee before they were anywhere near the lease. God, he hoped Bodin was one of the good guys. He was even starting to like him. They didn't need to do another flyover, so they only scouted drop-off and pick-up locations before Bodin landed at the first target area. Aaron caught the two giving each other heated looks before he ducked out of the helicopter.

Aaron and Elle walked a ways in silence before he asked, "All teasing aside, how are you this morning?"

Elle glanced at him as they walked through the forest. "Incredible. I didn't know it could be like that between two people."

Aaron studied her and knew she was telling the truth. He relaxed a bit. Bodin was bigger than he was. It would really suck to have to punch him out. Elle must have read the expression on his face and tugged at his arm.

"Come on, my sweet, adopted, protective, older brother. We've got work to do." She was quiet a moment before adding, "Thanks though."

Aaron slung an arm around her shoulder and planted a kiss on the top of her head. "No problem. Let's go find some sites." He let go and they continued walking.

****

Some distance from the helicopters, Bodin was lying on the soft reindeer moss covering the ground. The day was bright. He could see a few clouds through the sparse canopy of the mature spruce forest. He caught himself thinking of Elle. Again. She was extraordinary. Not just in bed, but in hundreds of different ways. The way she moved and carried herself, her intelligence, her sense of humor–in everything, she was extraordinary to him. The way she had diffused his hot temper yesterday morning with a few well-chosen words and determined attitude was amazing in itself. He wasn't known for being easy to deal with. To be honest, he was usually an asshole. Angels avoided him whenever possible. That should say something.

He had watched her go over the maps with Aaron, choosing target areas, weighing the potential of an area to yield an archaeology site within the confines of the project. He could tell she was good at what she did. Bodin had been fascinated watching the wheels of her quick, efficient mind spin.

Then, of course, there was last night. It had been incredible. Sure, the sex had been absolute, but it was more than that. He wanted to hold her every night. Wake up every morning to her beautiful face. She had made him laugh this morning. Bodin hadn't remembered what laughing felt like because it had been so long. Her unselfconscious nature had inspired him to discard the habitual urge to scowl and the armor of stubbornness. He had given himself to the laughter this morning, and to her. Bodin never wanted to let go. She had breathed life back into him. He felt more alive now than he had before he became a Changeling.

He wanted to show her in a thousand different ways how much she meant to him. He wanted to experience life, with her. Life actually looked worth living, and she had opened so many doors for him. He had never met a mortal woman who consumed his attention so completely. Gaia did, albeit in a more maternal, non-carnal sort of way. But she was the Divine, for crying out loud.

Bodin was so wrapped up in thoughts, he did not sense or hear Michael's approach.

"Everyone has the Divine spark in them, but you're right, Elle's is certainly brighter than most. Makes sense, she reminds you of Gaia," Michael said as he walked up.

Bodin started, jumped, and crouched, prepared for battle.

"At ease. It's just me," Michael said.

"Make some noise next time," Bodin snapped, but stood up and allowed the tension to drain from him. He was angry with himself for having not noticed Michael sooner.

"Daydream with half your mind next time so the other half can be alert."

"And quit reading my mind," Bodin roared.

"Quit leaving it wide open like a blasted book," Michael shot back.

Bodin opened his mouth to hurl an answer but shut it. Michael was right. He was all mixed up since he met Elle. That could be dangerous in his line of work. Angels had a stereotype, with some, of being lovey-dovey, with pretty feathers and singing choruses. Few knew it was hard, often dangerous work, especially for Changelings. They had the Achilles' heel of still being part human.

"Am I off the assignment?" Bodin asked, unable to keep the forlorn tone out of his voice. Crap, he was getting soft. First a wussy voice. What was next, breaks for a freakin' tea party?

"Enough." Michael commanded. He whistled softly. "You fell hard."

Bodin recovered enough to glare at Michael.

"That's better, back to glaring. And the answer is, no, you are not off the assignment. The assignment has been modified."

Bodin felt a glimmer of hope.

"Your assignment is to get to know her."

Bodin stared at Michael. "That's not an assignment."

"True, it is not a typical one, but you're not a typical Changeling. Gaia's losing patience with you and has threatened to pull out whatever stick you shoved up your ass that is blocking you from evolving and advancing as a Divine Being. Her words, not mine, so you can quit glowering at me. You are to do some serious soul searching, as well as get to know Elle. She's a human, yes, but you've had a thousand years, and you haven't figured out how to love and receive love from us. Elle's quite lovable and won't take your grumpy crap, either."

"Does she know she's on assignment, too?" Bodin

challenged, when what he was really thinking was just how lovable Elle was.

"Her soul and subconscious mind do. Gaia visited her a couple nights ago in Dream Scape. Her conscious mind couldn't quite recall the dream, although she remembered she had one. That is more than most people who have divine conversations in Dream Scape."

Bodin glowered at Michael. "I'm not in love with her, you know."

Michael waited patiently, saying nothing.

"I just wanted to get in her pants." Bodin balked at his own crass, lewd words. It was more than that, and he knew it to the very depths of his soul.

"Don't be such an ass. You blow this and it will haunt you forever. More than Eric's death ever could."

"Is that a threat?" Bodin snarled.

"It's the truth. You've been a stagnant pain in the ass for eons. Move on, kid. Your energy is too tied up in the past, and everybody is bloody sick of it. For the millionth time, release it! Move forward! Gaia hasn't given up on you, but I'm ready to drop-kick your spoiled ass and let Artemis use it for target practice."

Bodin took a step back. Michael actually looked disgusted. Bodin had never heard Michael speak so harshly or ever heard rumor about it. After all these years, he didn't know Michael did that or even could do that. He had pushed the archangel too far.

"I'm sorry," Bodin said quietly. "And you're right," he said with conviction. Somehow, he had been given a second chance, more like a billion chances, and he had the feeling his time was about up. Shit or get off the pot, he thought, remembering the corny but effective phrase. He had the sinking feeling he had wasted a thousand years being a stubborn, petulant child.

"I'm here if you need me," Michael said. "You just have to call."

Still ashamed, Bodin nodded. Michael punched him in the arm lightly. "Suck it up. So it took you a thousand years. Could have been longer."

Bodin gave a half smile. "Yeah. I guess. Uh, Michael?"

"Yes?"

"Thanks," Bodin said sincerely.

Michael nodded. "You know how to find me." And then he disappeared.

Bodin stood still, absorbing the enormity of what had just happened. He felt the thick, giant shell he had entombed himself in crack. He felt the enormous weight of it clearly for the first time and collapsed on his hands and knees, desperate to throw off the oppressive, crushing weight.

He took deep, gulping breaths of air and willed the weight to be gone, to disappear. He struggled as images of his past wrestled with him, trying to pull him back under. Scenes of himself, his past choices, convictions, ignorance, and untruths, assaulted him. He battled the circumstances, ideals, and responsibilities that had been thrust upon him, both by himself and others. He fought and struggled and strained against the shackles he had locked himself up with, until he was exhausted and wondered, for the first time, if he was going to make it, or if he had dug himself in too deep.

He heard someone calling his name. It was muted, at first, from a distance. Then it gained strength. He had rolled onto his back at one point and now rolled his head in the direction of the sweet voice. Elle was running to him, frantic. She had come for him. She would save him. He felt her pull, her radiating warmth and love. For the first time in his life, he allowed himself to be loved. It wasn't the love of lust or possession, it was pure, honest love, one being to another. No strings, no restrictions, just a strength so powerful and pure it broke Bodin free of the dark place he had built for himself. He grasped Elle when she dropped to her knees beside him.

****

"Are you okay? What's wrong? Are you hurt? What's going on?"

Tears were streaming down Elle's cheeks. Aaron watched her trained hands run over Bodin as she checked for injuries. They all had first aid training, it was a requirement for fieldwork.

"What's going on? What happened?" Elle cried as she worked.

Aaron had also raced across the clearing at the sight of Bodin seemingly lifeless, something had to be very wrong. Aaron read Bodin's energy pattern. It was in chaos. His energy was in overdrive and all over the place. Bodin was in danger of short-circuiting. He needed grounding, and he needed it now.

Aaron knelt immediately and wrapped his arms around Bodin's feet and lower legs. He hoped Elle would understand. She had no idea of his unusual talent, and Aaron wasn't looking forward to the conversation. He quickly asked the earth and surrounding forest for backup in a quick prayer, then began channeling the excess energy Bodin had swarming through him. Aaron felt everything Bodin had just experienced but from the safety of being solidly grounded and with the earth and forest's support. He was blown away by the emotional power pouring from Bodin and storming through him before he neutralized it in the forgiving soil.

Finally, the storm broke, leaving Bodin panting and Aaron exhausted.

"What just happened?" Elle was shaking slightly, her face devoid of all color.

Aaron saw the fright in Elle's eyes and couldn't blame her. There had been arcs of light going from Bodin, through Aaron, and then disappearing into the ground. He took a steadying breath, then another. He had never channeled that much energy before. Bodin must have gone through the wringer with that much energy. Elle stared at the two men, waiting.

Chapter Eleven

"I'm a Diffuser. What's your excuse?" Aaron said, trying to lighten the intense mood and knowing it was futile. It had been a hell of a few minutes. Bodin seemed okay; that was a relief. Aaron turned to see how Elle was taking it. Not well, he would guess, by the expression on her face.

"Changeling," Bodin answered. He sounded resigned.

"Diffuser? Changeling? Someone please start talking, and fast," Elle said in a strained voice.

Aaron knew she was trying desperately to remain calm, but she was scared. To be fair, though, her best friend had just acted like a conductor for the energy spewing from the man she had recently become quite intimate with. Aaron watched her grab her water bottle like it was a lifeline. Her hands were shaking as she took a long pull from it. She lowered the bottle, still trembling.

"I'm a Diffuser. I can see energy and am allowed to manipulate it in certain situations. Bodin was trying to rid himself of excess energy. That's why I was allowed to help."

Aaron ran his hand through the moss in a distracted gesture. "It's a bit more complicated, but that's the quick explanation. It's an ancient, hereditary skill, passed on paternally. Few know about it, anymore. It had to go underground for centuries. We live in different times now, but my dad and grandfather are hesitant for it to get out."

Aaron saw how hurt she was. "It's not exactly dinner

conversation, Elle. What was I supposed to say? Besides, people have gotten hurt in the past, knowing. I can't let anything happen to you, on account of me."

"You could have told me." She sniffed. "Not scare the hell out of me. Surely, *sometime* in the past, it could have come up."

"That's just it. I didn't want to scare you. Please understand, Elle. I never want to see you hurt, and I knew this had the potential." Even Aaron heard the pleading in his own voice. It was so important for her to understand, though.

"I trust you. I know you, so I know you must have thought it important not to share that completely huge part of your life."

Elle exhaled before she shoved his shoulders in mock anger. Aaron fell the short distance to a prone position. She was looming over him and smacking his shoulder. "Don't you ever keep a secret like that from me again. You hear me?"

Aaron stayed down, hesitant, until she ordered him to get over there and give her a hug. He immediately sat up and folded Elle into his arms. "Thanks, Elle." He was grateful for her trust in him, and their friendship.

****

Bodin watched the two friends and wondered if Elle would accept him as readily as she accepted Aaron. The two had a long history, which helped. Bodin wanted to have a chance to make one with Elle. Hell, he wouldn't mind an actual friend in Aaron, either, and not just because the guy had saved his life. No one since Eric had ever gotten as close to him as Elle and Aaron had been able to do in just a couple of days. Bodin patiently waited, perhaps for the first time in his life. If Elle's reaction was bad, he was in no hurry to receive it. Really, who wanted to hook up with a lightning rod? He hoped she would. He watched her pull Aaron in for one more relieved hug, and then she turned her attention on him.

Bodin's shoulders slumped. His time was likely up. "I'm a Changeling, which is someone who was once a human and is in training to be an angel." They stared at him in stunned silence. "It's true, although I suck at it. Too much of an ass," Bodin said, trying for humor. Another first in his life. Clearly he wasn't very good at that either.

Elle's face was contorted in shock and shame. "I had *sex* with an angel?" she asked, horrified. "Isn't that cosmically illegal or something? An angel? How is that even possible?" She started to tremble again and appeared completely disgusted with herself.

"I'm still very much part-human," Bodin said quietly, desperately wanting to reach for her. She didn't say anything else. She just stared at the ground, absorbing everything that had happened, that had been said.

"I'm still the same Bodin."

No response.

"Why can't you look at me, Elle? I'm still the same guy."

She sat with her knees huddled to her chest, her arms wrapped tight around them, not saying anything. He could feel her withdrawing into herself. He turned to Aaron, not knowing what to say.

Aaron angled his head in the direction away from Elle. The two men walked away a short distance before Aaron spoke, "Give her time. We've dropped a lot on her today. She'll come around. She's never lit up for anyone like she has for you."

Bodin wasn't so sure, but his only option was hoping Aaron was right.

"Are you okay to fly us back?" Aaron asked.

Bodin did a quick scan of his body and wasn't surprised at the reading. There wasn't a chance in hell he could fly that helicopter back to camp. He felt like he had electrocuted himself with his own energy. He would have to call Michael for help. "I'll take care of it."

"I'll go tell Elle we're heading back to camp. Let us know when you are ready."

Bodin nodded. He felt hollow. He was finally free of the shell he had been carrying for so long. But without Elle sharing her light with him anymore, he was empty. He walked away, heading a few steps into the surrounding forest. Part of him wished he had never been on this assignment, had never met Elle. Old habits died hard, and he found himself erecting walls again, rebuilding the shell he had shed at such a cost. Remembering his weakened state and that he needed Michael's help, he called his boss and mentor. Michael appeared immediately.

"That was fast," Bodin commented without inflection.

"I never left."

"Why didn't you do something?" Bodin protested, hurting more than he thought possible.

"You know the answer to that," Michael said with compassion in his eyes.

Bodin felt deflated and alone. He just wanted to shrink from the world. He nodded. "Can we just go?"

****

Elle looked up when she heard them approaching and blinked. Bodin's boss was walking next to him. Could this day get any more bizarre? Aaron appeared surprised for a heartbeat before he recovered.

"Ready to go?" He asked.

"Yes. You guys have already met Michael. He'll fly us in. I can't yet," Bodin answered before opening the helicopter door and climbing in.

Elle watched him move. He was hurt, but trying to hide it. How could she not have noticed earlier? She longed to reach out to him but stopped herself. He felt a million miles away. Elle climbed into the backseat of the helicopter with Aaron and turned to her best friend. She had no idea what to say. Aaron reached out and squeezed her hand before buckling in.

She was grateful for his support, but she deserved a kick in the pants instead. She had totally blown it with Bodin. Sure, she had received two shocks today, three if she counted the energy display earlier, but that was no excuse for the way she had treated him. He was right. He was the same Bodin she'd met on the plane, the same Bodin she had laughed with, the same one she had scolded. The same one she'd had hard, fast sex with, and slow, sweet loving, too. The same one she had fallen in love with.

That really was it. She was in love with him. Stubborn, cranky, gorgeous, irresistible Bodin.

Chapter Twelve

The ride back to camp was miserable. Elle kept replaying the events over in her head and wishing she had done things differently. There were a million ways she could have dealt with things better. Elle could see the front seat and the back of Bodin's neck. She wanted to caress that neck and wipe away the hurt and pain she had put in his eyes. She was glad she could not see them right now, though. She needed to gather more courage before she faced those hard, green, beautiful eyes again.

In the last few days, she had seen herself through his eyes. She had never known that she possessed such confidence, grace, laughter, and actual sex appeal before. Maybe she didn't. Bodin brought those things out in her. That grumpy man brought out so much beautiful in her. She wished she could say she did the same for him.

Elle gazed out the window and tried to escape the painful emotions swirling inside the helicopter. Her eye caught the large, impressive shape of a bear. It was peering up at the helicopter. Her brow puzzled into a wrinkle. That didn't make sense. Wildlife ran from helicopters. It didn't stop and ogle them. The hair on the back of Elle's neck stood up in warning. Something primitive inside her shuddered. That was no ordinary bear. She tried to shake off the odd feeling and was relieved they would be back at camp soon.

Bodin did not meet Aaron and Elle for dinner like he had before. Elle picked at her food more than actually ate any of it.

"Are we good?" Aaron asked.

Elle looked up, startled out of her thoughts. "What? Oh yeah, we're good."

"So your loss of appetite is not from pining over me?" he continued with a half-smile.

"Nice try, but no," Elle answered, mustering up her own half smile and pushing the food around her plate another lap.

"Go talk to him. His room is E10."

Her head snapped up. "How do you know that?"

"We had a beer this afternoon," Aaron answered with a shrug.

"Beer? You two had beers? Why didn't you invite me?" She was enraged and hurt.

"Why didn't we invite you? It's not rocket science. You said you wanted to be alone after we got back. We left you alone."

Elle lowered her head. She had snapped a bit in declaring her alone time. "Well, that sounds way more fun than the wallowing in self-pity I did this afternoon."

"That's the Elle I know and love. Go talk to him."

She hesitated for a moment, then smiled. "I think I will," she sprang from her chair at the table and almost knocked it down in her excitement and haste. Now that she had made up her mind to go, she wanted to be there immediately. Patience was not her strong suit.

"Easy," he said and laughed. "I have something for you before you go."

She gave a dramatic sigh and grinned. "Well, hurry up, already."

Aaron laughed as he pulled a box out of his kit bag and slid it across the table towards her. Elle's cheeks colored when she identified the box of condoms careening towards her. She snatched the box with amazing speed.

"Aaron!" Her tone was full of censure, but she rounded the table to kiss his cheek and throw her arms around him. "Thank you! We were nearly out!"

She hit him with such speed and enthusiasm that he started tipping from his chair. His arm went around her to stop them both from falling.

"Take it easy, woman. Geez, Bodin's one lucky dude," Aaron said grinning.

Elle laughed and snatched for his kit bag.

"What are you doing? I don't have any more in there. You must be insatiable." Aaron made a grab for the kit bag.

She held it out of reach and discreetly slid the box of condoms inside. "I'm not walking down the hall of any camp with a big ol' box of condoms. I'll give you your kit bag later." She winked. "See you!"

Elle dashed off and nearly collided with Bodin.

****

Instinctively, Bodin caught Elle. She had slipped trying to shift her weight to avoid running smack into him. He held on an extra second, then two, before forcing himself to let her go. He had seen the interchange between her and Aaron when he walked into the cafeteria. Bodin was hurt, pissed off, and, Goddess help him, still had trouble releasing her arms after she had steadied herself. He had trusted her—hell, he'd trusted Aaron, too—that there was nothing going on between them. It sure didn't appear like nothing. How could she fuck his brains out last night and be kissing Aaron today?

"Bodin, hi! I was just coming to find you!" Elle said

with excitement.

He glared at her with the daggers he was feeling. "Yeah, right."

She looked confused and hurt. "Of course I was. Aaron said I should go talk to you—" She stopped abruptly. "Oh, uh…you don't want to talk to me. I understand."

Elle started to back away and he saw her face start to crumple. She pressed her white-knuckled fist against the bridge of her nose, visibly trying not to lose the last of her composure.

Aaron stomped up and pinned Bodin with an irritated stare. "Quit looking at me like that, numb nuts, before you make an even bigger ass of yourself. And Elle, for god sakes, buck up. Why in the hell are you backing away?" Aaron asked, scowling. He picked up his fallen kit bag and slapped it into her hands. "Go. Take the damn bag." He stalked away, muttering something about clueless twits.

****

Bodin sat on the bed and scowled while Elle paced the room. She was wringing her hands like she was nervous. She had practically dragged him here. He had wanted to bolt.

She stopped abruptly and blurted, "Are you mad about the field? Because I acted weird? But why would you be mad at Aaron, too?" She was getting worked up again. "You two hit me with Mack trucks today. Do you hear me? Freakin' Mack trucks. And since when are you and Aaron all chummy? You could have invited me for beers today. That was pretty rude. I mean, you guys don't even like each other. And why does Aaron keep waving that spoon at you? I don't get it. You guys haven't known each other long enough to have inside jokes yet, and he won't tell me."

Horrified, Elle realized she wanted to stomp her foot in frustration. "And to top it all off, I realized on that stupid ride back today that I think I'm falling in love with you." She sniffled and, rubbing her nose, prayed she wouldn't break down and cry again. "I know that's stupid, but I can't help it. Now you know." Mortified, she covered her face with her hands. She couldn't believe she told him. What was she thinking? She just kept screwing up with him.

Bodin watched her with fascination and hope, and his scowl quickly turned into a smile. He stood and walked over to her. He pulled her hands away from her face and kissed her.

"You're not mad?" Elle asked, hopeful. She was holding onto his hands and not letting go.

"A misunderstanding is all," he murmured and started kissing her again.

Elle grabbed his shirt and, kissing him back, pushed him back against the bed and then down on it. She seductively crawled up his body and took her time to kiss and nip as she went. She stopped, pulled at Aaron's kit bag, tugged the box of condoms out, and dropped them on his stomach. "A present from Aaron to the happy couple."

Bodin looked at the box. "I'm an ass. No wonder you were excited."

"Yeah, on both counts. Want to have our first make-up sex?" Elle murmured, starting to trail kisses all over him again.

Bodin growled in satisfaction and wrapped his arms around her.

Chapter Thirteen

Bodin dropped Elle and Aaron off the next morning. He was still hot from the hungry glance she had tossed him before she hopped out of the helicopter. The night had sizzled between them, and by morning, nothing had cooled off. If anything, Bodin was hungrier. They had taken a shower together, which, in hindsight, wasn't the brightest idea they'd had. Neither of them had been able to keep their hands off each other, and they were late meeting Aaron. Again. He had just smiled and drunk his coffee, asking for his kit bag back. Bodin had taken him aside while Elle was busy loading her gear and apologized for being an ass last night. Aaron took it in stride, as usual. He had just shrugged and said, "No worries," before loading his own gear.

Bodin landed at the next assigned meeting place and powered down the helicopter. He looked around him for a while. He had seen most of the world in the last thousand years. Landscapes had always called to him, even before he became a Changeling. He had traveled more than most in his thirty-six years before Eric died and he had taken up the Oath. Landscapes seemed more of a friend to him than most people ever had.

A sigh escaped him. He was tired of fighting himself. Tired of fighting Michael, Gaia, his assignments, everything. He wanted peace. He was ready for it for the first time in his life. Bodin felt lighter with the realization. His thought turned to Elle—sweet, beautiful, smart, sassy, honest Elle.

She had turned his life upside down. More than that, she had saved his life. Her simple presence made happiness seem possible for him. He had never really believed it existed. Sure, he had seen people who appeared happy, had had assignments that helped make people happy. But he had never believed that could be a lifestyle, a state of mind, an actual existence. He never knew it was possible to see yourself honestly and be happy with who you saw. To have people actually happy that you were in their life was a potent thing.

He saw it this morning. He'd awakened to Elle's smiling face, her eyes dancing, happy to see him, touch him, know him. She made him believe he still had a soul. She gave him hope for life, for the future, for himself. He saw himself through her eyes and saw goodness for the first time. She loved him. How about that? He had wasted so many opportunities to believe in love. His job for the last ten eons had revolved around love and he had never given the emotion, the feeling, the power, the reverence it deserved.

Love truly is Divine. He knew that now. He had felt Divine for the first time in his life sometime in the middle of the night. Elle had enveloped him in her embrace and he felt the full force of her love emanate from her into him. It was incredible. He felt connected to the whole Divine universe for that split second. He knew he was part of it, not a bystander scowling from the sidelines but an active, worthy, viable participant in life. Hell, even Aaron was warming to him. Bodin liked the guy. Soon, he might even be able to admit it to other people.

He quickly finished his paperwork. Even Changelings posing as helicopter pilots had to fill out corporate paperwork. *It shouldn't be more than an hour before they showed up, long enough for a catnap.* He stretched and opened the helicopter door.

Bodin felt a little bad Elle wouldn't have the luxury of a nap after their second sex marathon last night. He was beat and was sure she was too. He hopped out, stretched again and noticed a very fresh pile of bear scat. With a sinking feeling, he felt the hairs on his nape quiver. He had felt that same quiver a few times each year since he became a Changeling. Bodin had never identified it, but it scared the shit out of him. Few things did, so he tended to pay attention to those that did.

He scanned the surrounding forest. Nothing appeared unusual. He wasn't sure what he was looking for but he checked just the same. The uneasy feeling started to intensify. Bodin started to get antsy. He felt his energy start to gather, like a storm building. Restless now, with no desire or ability to take a nap, he started pacing the perimeter of the clearing. Getting nervous and a bit frustrated, he called out to Elle and Aaron on the radio, but only static met his inquiry.

He tried calling Elle's cell phone. Some of the leases had cell phone towers on them to facilitate operations. He hoped they were close enough to one to get a signal. After trying both Elle's and Aaron's with no luck, he tried texting them. Sometimes text messages went through when phone calls couldn't. He waited a minute for a response. Nothing.

Thinking, wondering what he should do, Bodin stalked back to the helicopter. The feeling of trepidation was getting stronger. He summoned Michael. A minute passed. Then five. Then fifteen. Bodin was getting frantic and pissed off. Michael was omnipresent. Where the hell was he? The feeling of danger was urgent now. Bodin didn't want to blink to where ever Michael, or even Gaia,

was and leave Elle and Aaron alone with whatever was
sending his senses into overdrive.

****

Michael watched Gaia. "I really don't like this part,
you know."

"I know. Sometimes people opt for the hard road,
though, for their lessons and experiences," Gaia answered
compassionately.

Michael nodded. This was the part he always hated,
when people asked for help, but it was in their best interests
not to have any help swoop in, but to ride out whatever was
going on. All he could do was send loving energy. He knew
it was necessary, just like last time. But, sometimes the
hiccups and hang time until things fell into place were hard
on everyone involved.

He was pleased Gaia's power play had produced
results so fast. Bodin's evolution was going at warp speed.
The Changeling had learned and grown and changed so
much in the last few days. More than he had in the
millennia prior. Bodin was happy and in love. Before, he
hadn't even believed they existed.

Michael and Gaia waited in silence, knowing what
was about to happen, knowing it needed to happen. Letting
it happen.

****

Elle rolled her eyes at Aaron. "You can't be serious.
Daniel Craig makes a way cooler Bond."

Aaron shrugged. "He's good, but I'm old school. I
still like Connery."

Elle laughed at him, "You're old school, all right. Which birthday is coming up again?"

"Quiet."

"Just because . . ."

"Quiet!" Aaron commanded, holding up his hand to stop her.

She heard something then, too. A large bear came charging through the bush and lunged for Aaron. Elle watched in horror as the enormous bear tackled her best friend. Without thought for her own safety, she swung her shovel at the bear. Her arms jarred when the shovel made contact with the hulking beast. The bear barely flinched but kept right on clawing and biting at Aaron. Elle hammered away, striking countless times at the bear. Tears were streaming down her face while she fought with all her might. A horrible, piercing cry screamed through the air. She didn't have time to register the apocalyptic sound when the bear suddenly swung around and lunged for her. Shrieking out of the way, Elle landed a potent blow to the bear's face with the shovel, stunning it as its head snapped to the side.

****

Bodin saw Elle hammering away at the berserk bear, and his heart splintered. In the quarter second it took to register what was going on, he knew what he had to do. It was the only way to save them in time. He loved her. Without hesitation, Bodin claimed his wings and took flight on a roar.

Chapter Fourteen

Bodin watched Elle lean over Aaron, gripping his hand in both of hers. She was on the ground, kneeling beside his prone body. Finally, he came to and asked, "Do I feel like a bear just mauled me because a bear just mauled me?"

Elle tried to smile at Aaron's humor. "Yes, and yes," she said as a few persistent tears escaped her control. Aaron would have been dead if it wasn't for Bodin. She might have been dead, too.

She had glanced up when Bodin, with a pair of ethereal wings, snatched her and Aaron into the air, away from the dangerous bear. Aaron's limp body had dangled from Bodin's strong grasp. Elle had clung to Bodin's free arm. She had watched, stunned, as he navigated them through the air and away from the bear, and out of danger. She had seen the predatory bear bow its head and disappear. She had blinked and checked again, but the bear was gone.

Aaron's handsome face was torn in several places. His clothes were shredded in various angles, his strong body bloodied and bruised. "Come on," she said. "We have to get out of here, once we know we can move you."

"He's not coming back," Bodin said quietly and handed Elle the first aid kit he must have found in either her or Aaron's bag. She was grateful for having to always lug the thing around, and for the work-required first aid training. As a team, Bodin and Elle finished checking Aaron over and assessing his injuries. They started to field dress the worst of his cuts.

"What, do you read bears' minds now?" Elle said sarcastically. She wrapped a bandage over Aaron's right bicep and tied the knot tight. She had no idea why she was giving Bodin attitude. He had saved them both. With big 'ol wings, no less. Reality was a distant memory since she'd met him.

Aaron turned toward her, surprised. "Did I miss something? Why are you mad at him? Hey, oww!"

"Sorry. I didn't mean to hurt you," she said, distracted, but tried for more delicacy on the next bandage. She ignored his question about Bodin.

"I know who he is." Bodin tied off another bandage.

"Who he is? It's a bear. Not a person," Elle said, not understanding Bodin and knowing she would not like his answer. "Aaron, quit moving," she snapped. "Sorry. Sorry. Fuck, I'm on a hair trigger right now."

"Let's get Aaron back to camp and checked out by the medic," Bodin said gently, ignoring her question. He then turned toward Aaron. "It looks like you only have cuts and bruises. Some are deep, but all should be manageable. And—"

"And check for internal injuries. It's okay. I know the drill."

Bodin gave Aaron a half smile. Its warmth didn't reach anywhere near his eyes. "I'm pretty sure you're going to be just fine. We'll just make sure. We can finish talking at camp."

Bodin's face stopped Elle. She had never seen such complete and utter sorrow. The sarcasm of a moment before ripped at her. Something way worse than a bear attack had just happened. She was scared to find out what, but she was more scared of losing Bodin to whatever darkness was gripping him. All the light had gone out of his eyes.

She grabbed his hands. "What is it? What happened?"

Looking defeated, he shook his head. "Let's just go."

****

For the second time, Elle rode back to camp feeling as though she had lost Bodin. She sat in the back of the helicopter with Aaron. He was alert and appeared stable, but the guy had just gone a few rounds with a bear. She glanced again at Aaron to assure herself he was okay, before swinging her gaze to the back of Bodin's head. It was all she could see of him in the front seat. She wanted desperately to lean forward and touch him, let him know he wasn't alone, but he felt a million miles away. Again.

Her only consolation was the knowledge that if they could figure it out before, they could figure it out again. And that's just what they were going to do, she decided. He might have been alone in the past, but he wasn't alone anymore. As the thoughts came to her, she started perking up. Bodin would just have to accept she loved him, and that's all there was to it.

She smiled then, figuring no one had ever made Bodin do anything he didn't want to do. Browbeating someone to accept your love probably wasn't the typical approach, but nothing had been typical since meeting him. Feeling much better, Elle felt a fraction of the tension she was carrying released. It would be okay. Aaron was safe. She and Bodin would work things out. It would be okay. She hoped.

"Sorry I snapped," she said into her mouthpiece.

Aaron turned toward her and smiled before wincing at the pain. He squeezed her hand and said nothing before staring back out the window. Bodin's large shoulders lifted on a deep breath. Elle didn't think he was going to respond until his voice came over the headset.

"Elle, whatever happens, know I did fall in love with you."

Her eyes widened. She should be over the moon at his words, but they sounded more foreboding than romantic. Aaron shot her a questioning look. Crap, this was worse than she'd thought.

****

Aaron was ordered rest for several days with daily checkups by the medical staff, but other than that was fine. Elle and Bodin settled him into his room.

"And here's the remote." Elle handed Aaron the large remote. "Need anything else?" she asked, before giving him a gentle, spontaneous hug. "I'm so glad you're going to be okay." She sniffed and wiped away a stray tear.

Aaron gave her a quick hug. "I'm glad too. Now, you two kids shoo." He studied the remote and said, "Leave me to figure out how to get the naughty channels in peace."

"Yup, you're just fine," Elle said.

"Of course I am. Hey, after you guys have your talk and your make-up sex, or figure-out sex, could you bring me ice cream? Vanilla, with chocolate sauce and sprinkles, please," Aaron said, distracted, playing with the remote and TV.

"Sprinkles?" Elle asked and laughed.

"Yes, sprinkles. A guy has a brush with death, he remembers the joys of childhood."

Bodin had been quiet until now and cleared his throat, uncomfortable. He couldn't have sex with Elle. Not now, not ever again.

Aaron turned toward Bodin. "Will you fill me in later?"

He nodded.

"With all of it?" Aaron pressed.

Bodin gave a half smile. Aaron really did have a quicksilver mind. "Yes, with all of it."

He turned and saw the worried look on Elle's face. *She knows we're not talking about sex anymore. I wish we were.*

****

In her room, Elle and Bodin sat on the bed facing each other.

"There's a lot to tell." Bodin bowed his head in regret. Love had come too late for him. He still couldn't believe what had happened. He ran his fingers through his hair and tried to exhale. He was stunned and ashamed and confused. Aaron and Elle were innocents. Why had they been targeted? The enormity of what he had done was also starting to filter through. *I claimed my wings. I'm an angel.* Bodin knew he shouldn't, but he pulled Elle close, anyway, for one hard, last kiss.

She eagerly responded with a fervent, almost desperate kiss. Bodin wondered if she somehow knew what was coming. He was feeling rather desperate, himself.

He broke the kiss, breathing hard. He gave her neck and shoulder one last caress before pulling away. He rubbed his face with his large hands, hating what he had to say. "I had to claim my wings in order to use them to save you guys."

"Your wings. What does that mean?"

Bodin looked at her in sorrow. "It means I'm not a Changeling anymore. I'm an Angel. I can't be with you anymore." He bowed his head again and shuddered. No wonder he had avoided love for so long—he didn't know if he could survive it.

"What?" Elle whispered. "I hope I just heard you wrong. Please tell me I heard you wrong."

"Elle—" Bodin reached for her.

"No!" Elle interrupted and grabbed his hands, pumping them. "No! No! No! That can't be! We just found each other." Tears starting to roll down her cheeks.

He wiped them away with gentle hands. "I know. It feels like I've waited my whole life to find you. I don't want to go anywhere." He pulled her close again and kissed the top of her head. Life was crueler than he'd ever imagined.

"When do you have to go?" She asked softly.

"I'm not sure," Bodin said. "I never had any intention of claiming my wings, so I never paid attention to that part."

"You didn't?"

"No. I only became a Changeling to take my friend Eric's place, when he died. I never really got into being an angel. Drove me nuts, truth be told."

"Wait a minute. You claimed your wings, which you never wanted to do, to save Aaron's and my life?" Elle asked, sounding a bit strangled. "But that's forever, isn't it? You traded your life for ours?"

"Pretty much." He saw her look of guilt and quickly added, "Don't even think it! I'd do it again and again and again, to save you. It was my choice. Do you hear me? My choice!"

Someone knocked at the door. Bodin felt Michael's presence and grudgingly opened the door for his boss. He stared at Michael a moment before he opened the door wide enough to allow him in. Bodin turned around, sat on the bed, took Elle's hand, kissed it. It was a clear message to Michael—Bodin was Elle's, as far as he was concerned.

He was furious, but knew it likely wasn't Michael's fault. He needed answers about the bear, though, and Michael could give them to him. The archangel walked in and nodded at Elle. She stared in fascination through the tears still in her eyes. "When you said Michael was your boss, you meant *the* Michael? As in the Archangel Michael?"

"Yes." The archangel smiled. "I am that Michael. Good to see you again, Elle." Michael turned his gaze on Bodin, and it hardened a bit. "Before you say something you'll regret, let's go. We're meeting in Aaron's room."

Bodin, unsure what he felt toward the archangel, stared at Michael. But he needed to know what was going to happen to him, now, and he wanted answers about that damn bear.

****

Michael knocked on Aaron's door before opening it. Elle and Bodin followed him in. Bodin nodded to Aaron, who was still recovering in bed. His eye then caught the man sitting on a chair, next to Aaron's bed.

"Hello, Bodin." Eric's voice was warm. "It's been a long time."

"You!" Bodin roared, pointing his finger at the man he used to call his best friend. "I trusted you!" Bodin grabbed the smaller man by the shirt and dragged him up, off the chair, before slamming him against the wall. "I trusted you! How could you do that! I took your place as a Changeling. I tried to carry on your torch, and what do you do? You've haunted me for eons, attacked the only friends I've had since you, and cornered me to claim those fucking wings. I hate you, you hear me?" Bodin slammed the man against the wall again in emphasis. "I hate you!" Bodin let Eric drop to the floor in disgust. He turned on Michael, then. "Why is he here? I want him out of here, away from Elle and Aaron."

Eric picked himself up quickly. "Whew, still have your temper. Bodin, listen to me—"

"Shut up!" Bodin bellowed at Eric before glaring at Michael. "Well?"

Gaia appeared before Michael had a chance to answer him. "Calm down, Bodin." She rubbed her ears gracefully. "And stop bellowing. Eric has been following you since he died, trying to help you, you big oaf. So just calm down."

Bodin looked from Gaia to Eric in confusion.

"It's true," Eric said. "I have been following you since the day I died. You are so hardheaded! I didn't think it was possible for you to get more stubborn, but, well, you did...have been, for freaking centuries."

"Eric! Focus!" Bodin interrupted.

Eric gave a sheepish half smile. "Okay, I'm still the same on some things, too. Anyway, it wasn't your fault I died! It was an accident, so you can quit blaming yourself. And quit blaming Rosalin, and us being in love. Accidents happen. Even to Changelings. I knew I shouldn't have taken that horse, and I did anyway. I got myself thrown. No one else did. I didn't ask for help either. It was stupid, I know. But there you go."

"But—" Bodin started.

"But nothing. I had an accident and died. End of story." Now Eric smiled. "But it has a happy ending. A few, actually." Eric winked at Gaia.

"What do you mean?" Bodin asked.

"Rosalin lived a long and happy life, but never forgot or stopped loving me. We've been together on the Other Side since. Keeping watch over your sorry arse, I might add, among other things."

"You have?" Bodin asked, very aware of all the shit he had done over the centuries. "Rosalin, too? She should hate me."

"Rosalin, too," Eric answered compassionately. "And no, she doesn't hate you. She tried to talk me out of shape shifting. She feared it was the wrong approach with you. We've been following you all these years, but your guilt and fear have shadowed our presence. That's why you always got that uncomfortable feeling–it was when I showed up." Eric shook his head. "Do you know how hard it has been to help you?"

Bodin glanced at Michael and Gaia before he admitted, sheepishly, "I have an idea."

Michael laughed.

"So let me get this straight," Bodin said. "Gaia, Michael, you, and Rosalin have been working for a millennium, trying to get my sorry ass to believe in love?"

The three of them nodded and Gaia added, "There are more, dozens more, who helped, but you get the gist."

Bodin sat down and rubbed his face in his hands. "I've been an idiot, haven't I?"

"Yes," Michael and Eric answered in unison.

"It took a very special woman to make you believe." Gaia nodded at Elle.

Bodin watched Elle. She had been quiet since they had walked into the room. She now turned toward Gaia and whispered, "Are you who I think you are?"

The Goddess smiled warmly. "Yes, I am."

Elle was thoughtful for a moment. "What happens now?"

"What does happen now?" Bodin was certain he didn't want to hear the answer. He took Elle's hand. He didn't know how long he would have left to hold it.

"Did you give her the rose?" Gaia asked.

"What? Oh, no, sorry! I can't believe I forgot," Bodin stammered. "I can go get it."

"I've got it." Gaia handed the shimmering flower to Elle. "This is for you."

"What is it?" Elle sounded uncertain, and she was looking pensively at both Gaia and the rose. "It's beautiful. It's like Bodin's wings."

Gaia smiled again. "Yes, on both counts. It is made of the same thing. It's yours." She held it out to Elle.

Elle peered at the flower again. She didn't move. "I don't mean to be ungrateful, but can I exchange it?"

Gaia beamed. "For what?"

"Bodin. If he'll have me. I want Bodin. I know it's selfish, him being an angel and all, but he said he was really crappy at it." She took a deep breath before she said, "I love him."

"But you don't even know what the rose does or is for," Gaia said. "Don't you want to know?"

Elle shook her head. "No. Not unless it can somehow help Bodin and I to be together…if that's what he wants, too, I mean."

"Bodin?" Gaia asked, "What do you want?"

"I want Elle," he answered immediately. He turned

and took Elle's hands in his. "I love her."

Tears started to roll down Elle's face, and she threw her arms around him. He wrapped his arms around her and held tight, uncertain.

Gaia beamed again and nodded her head. "So be it." The room started to sparkle and spin and a loud whooshing sound ended on a thump.

"Ow!" Bodin growled, trying to rub his back at the slicing pain on his shoulder blades. "That hurt."

"I suppose I could have warned you," Gaia said with a wink and shrug.

"I deserved that. I've been a pain."

Gaia only nodded mildly in return.

Bodin turned toward Eric. "You were part of this, weren't you? I've been such an ass. You guys had to corner me to help me."

Eric nodded. Bodin went to his best friend and gave him a huge hug, thumping the smaller man on the back. Eric appeared startled, but recovered quickly.

"You're welcome." Shaking his head, Eric added, "A Changeling. I still can't believe you did it."

"We were like brothers. What else was I supposed to do?"

"What indeed?" Eric laughed. "I'm happy to have my best friend back. I can finally visit you in Dream Scape." Eric turned to Aaron. "I'm sorry about mauling you. I tried to make it look real, but not do too much damage."

"Not a problem." Aaron shrugged a shoulder. "Nothing that a few days and a little R&R can't take care of. It was worth it."

"That goes for you, too, Elle," Eric added sincerely. "I never wanted to hurt you guys. I just needed your help to help knucklehead here."

Elle snuggled back into Bodin's embrace. "I'm glad you did."

Bodin faced Michael and opened his mouth to say something, but nothing came out. He had no idea how to thank him.

Michael nodded. "I know."

"Don't make this easy on me," Bodin grumbled, completely humbled by everything that had happened. He was surrounded by beings who loved him. It shook him to the core. "Brothers?"

"Always," Michael answered.

Bodin looked at everyone in the room. "Thank you." He cleared his throat. A lump had suddenly formed there. "Am I good to go?" Bodin asked Gaia and Michael.

"You are." Gaia's eyes were shining.

"I'll keep in touch," Michael said. "You know, for old times' sake. I know how much you loved me checking up on you."

Bodin laughed. "You do that. Now, if you'll excuse us, we have to go ride our bikes. I remembered how." He swept Elle up into his arms and walked out of the room.

****

"They're going for a bike ride? Now?" Eric said, not understanding.

Michael's face lit up in merriment. "No, there're not actually going for a bike ride. Never mind."

"Well, that turned out pretty cool," Aaron said.

Michael turned to Aaron. "It was pretty cool you channeled that energy for Bodin."

Aaron shrugged. "It's what I do. Bodin can be an ass, but he really grew on me."

"It's more than that, and you know it. Thank you," Gaia said. "We'll keep in touch."

Aaron nodded. "I figured you would."

****

Hours later, Elle and Bodin lay wrapped in each other's arms. "Say it again." Elle giggled.

"I love you," Bodin said confidently. "It feels good to say the words. I love you, I love you." He kissed along her neck. "I love you. Love you here." More kisses. "And here."

This time, he kissed her ear, flicking his tongue inside. She shivered in anticipation.

"And here."

Bodin moved to her lips. Elle pulled away after a sizzling kiss. "I love you, too. Are you sure you're okay with what happened? I don't want to hold you back or corner you. You claimed your wings, well, kind of."

She looked hesitant and worried. Bodin held her even tighter. "You're what I want. I want to spend the rest of my life with you. You're amazing, Elle. I love you. You helped me to really live. I had a thousand years, and I didn't get it, until you. Forget the wings. I claimed love."

Elle closed her eyes a moment and soft tears escaped, but when she opened them, her smile was brilliant. She hugged him as tight as she could. "I want you forever. I love you. You brought out the real me. I had hidden her away, and you found her anyway. You coaxed her out. How did you do that?" She gave a soft unladylike sniffle and burrowed deeper into his embrace. "Never mind, it doesn't matter. Sounds like we're good for each other."

Bodin lifted his head. "Do you mean that?"

"Yes, I do."

"Marry me."

"Bodin, I was going to ask you!" Elle exclaimed and hugged him. "Oh my god, oh my god."

"So that's a yes, then? I know it's kind of soon, but —"

"Yes! Yes, yes, yes! It's not too soon. I love you so much." She snuggled close again and started kissing and playfully nipping his neck and ear.

"Bodin?" She asked innocently.

"Yeah?" He groaned a bit when Elle nipped at his earlobe. He tightened his arm around her.

"Do we have time for a quickie before we meet Aaron for supper? You know, to celebrate?"

Bodin pulled Elle on top of him, but not before she saw his pure, radiant smile. "Definitely."

Sarah Kades writes outdoor adventure and paranormal romances to celebrate love, the great outdoors, and to inspire others to go have their own adventures. She lives in Calgary, Alberta, Canada with her husband and daughter, the family dog and cat, and a house full of plants. When she is not writing, she can be found reading a good book or playing outside with her family and friends.

Visit her at www.sarahkades.com.

Happy Reading.